Paddington Abroad

Paddington Abroad

by
MICHAEL BOND

With drawings by
Peggy Fortnum

A YEARLING BOOK

Published by
Dell Publishing Co., Inc.
1 Dag Hammarskjold Plaza
New York, New York 10017

ISBN: 0-440-47352-7

Yearling ® TM 913705, Dell Publishing Co., Inc.
Reprinted by arrangement with Houghton Mifflin Company
Printed in the United States of America
Eighth Dell Printing—March 1980

CW

CONTENTS

Paddington Prepares

PADDINGTON WAS in a mess. As he was the sort of bear who often got himself into trouble he wasn't really surprised—but as he stood up and looked round his bedroom even he had to admit that it was worse than usual.

There were maps and pieces of paper everywhere, not to mention several nasty-looking marmalade stains and a long trail of paw prints. The paw prints started on a map which was spread across the eiderdown on his bed. It was a large map of London and in the middle, by the first paw mark, there was a circle which marked the position of the Browns' house at No. 32 Windsor Gardens.

The trail led from the Browns' house across the map in a southerly direction, over the end of the bed and on to another map which lay on the floor at the foot. From there it carried on, still going south, until it reached the English Channel, and yet a third map by the window which showed the north coast of France. There the trail ended in a soggy mess made up of old cake crumbs, a small pile of marmalade and a blob of red ink.

Paddington gave a deep sigh as he dipped his paw absent-mindedly into the concoction. He tried kneeling on the floor and peering at his room through half-closed eyes, but if anything, the mess looked even worse because from so low down all he could see were the bumps and ridges.

Just as he was about to lie back and consider the matter he was suddenly brought back to life by the sound of clinking plates and footsteps on the stairs.

Jumping up with a guilty expression on his face, Paddington hurriedly began sweeping everything under the bed. Although he had some very good explanations for the mess he was in he felt sure neither Mrs. Brown nor Mrs. Bird would be very keen on hearing them—especially at breakfast time when everyone was usually in a great hurry.

" Are you awake, Paddington? " called Mrs. Brown as she knocked on the door.

" No—not yet, Mrs. Brown," cried Paddington in a muffled voice, as he tried to push his marmalade jar under the wardrobe. " I think my lids are stuck."

Being a truthful bear at heart, Paddington closed his eyelids and snored several times while he gathered up the rest of his belongings. Feeling around for the pen and ink, he hastily put them into his old hat which he pulled down over his head, and then, gathering up the last of the maps, he groped his way across the room.

" Whatever's going on, Paddington? " exclaimed Mrs. Brown, as the door suddenly opened and Paddington appeared.

Paddington nearly fell over backwards with surprise when he saw Mrs. Brown standing there with his breakfast tray.

" I thought you were a cupboard, Mrs. Brown," he exclaimed, as he hurriedly put a pawful of maps behind him and backed towards the bed. " I must have gone the wrong way by mistake."

" I should think you did," said Mrs. Brown as she followed him into the room. " I've never heard so much banging and crashing."

Mrs. Brown looked suspiciously round the room but everything appeared to be in its place so she turned her attention back to Paddington who was now sitting up in bed with a very odd expression on his face.

" Are you sure you're all right? " she asked anxiously, as she placed the tray in front of him. For one nasty moment Mrs. Brown thought she saw a trickle of red running down Paddington's left ear, but before she could look into the matter he had pulled his old hat even further down over his head. All the same she didn't like the look of it at all, and she hesitated at the door in case something was wrong.

Paddington, in his turn, rather wished Mrs. Brown would hurry up and go. In his haste to clear up the mess he had forgotten to put the stopper back on the bottle of ink and the top of his head was beginning to feel quite soggy.

Mrs. Brown sighed as she closed the door. She knew from past experience that it was hopeless trying to get an explanation out of Paddington when he was in one of his difficult moods.

" If you ask me," said Mrs. Bird, when Mrs. Brown joined her in the kitchen and told her all about Paddington's strange behaviour, " that young bear isn't the only one in this house who's acting in a funny manner. It's all to do with *you know what*! "

With that Mrs. Brown had to agree. Things had been very much upside down in the Brown household ever since the previous evening.

It had all started when Mr. Brown arrived home carrying a large pile of maps and brightly coloured pamphlets and announced that he was taking them to France for their summer holiday.

In a matter of moments the normal peace and quiet of No. 32 Windsor Gardens had disappeared completely never to return.

The holiday had been the one topic of conversation from dinner time until last thing at night. Old beach balls and bathing-costumes had been searched for in disused cupboards, plans had been discussed, and Mrs. Bird had already begun washing and ironing a small mountain of clothes ready for the big day.

Paddington in particular had been most excited at the news. Since he had been a member of the Brown family they had taken him on a number of day trips which he had enjoyed no end, but he had never before been away for a real holiday and he was looking forward to it. To add to his excitement Mr. Brown, in a generous moment, had put him in charge of all the maps and a thing called an itinerary.

At first Paddington hadn't been at all sure about being in charge of anything which sounded so important as an itinerary, but after Judy had explained to him that it was simply a list of all the places they would visit and the things they would do he had quickly changed his mind. Paddington was keen on lists and a " doings list " sounded most interesting.

" Mind you," said Mrs. Bird darkly, as she discussed the matter with Mrs. Brown over the washing-up, " if that young bear's going to be in charge of the maps we shall need all of a fortnight. It's asking for trouble. There's no knowing where we might end up."

Mrs. Brown sighed again. " Oh, well," she said,

turning her attention to other things, "at least it keeps him happy. You know how keen he is on writing things."

"H'mm!" said Mrs. Bird. "It'll be all over the sheets if I know anything. Itineraries indeed!"

She snorted and cast a dark glance up at the ceiling in the direction of Paddington's room on the second floor.

Mrs. Bird knew from past experience and much washing of sheets that ink and Paddington were two things best kept apart. But as it happened for once she needn't have worried for Paddington had just that moment stopped writing. In fact he was sitting up in bed carefully studying a large sheet of drawing-paper which he held in his paws.

At the top of the paper in big, red capital letters was the heading:

EYETINNERY BY PADINGTUN

followed by his special paw mark to show that it was genuine.

Paddington wasn't quite sure about the spelling of itinerary, but though he had looked through all the E's in Mr. Brown's dictionary the night before he hadn't been able to find it anywhere. On the whole, Paddington wasn't surprised. He didn't think much of dictionaries and he often found that when he wanted to look up a particularly difficult word it was nowhere to be found.

The first item on the list was:—

7 *oh clock*—Large Breckfast

and then came

8 *oh clock*—Leeve Home (32 Windsor Gardens)
9 *oh clock*—Snak
11 *oh clock*—Elevenses

Paddington read through the list several more times and then, after adding the words 12 *oh clock—arrive at Airplane—Lunch*, he folded the paper and packed it away in the secret compartment of his suitcase. Planning a holiday—especially a holiday abroad—was much more complicated than he had imagined, and he decided the only thing to do was to consult his friend Mr. Gruber on the subject.

A few minutes later, after a quick wash, he hurried downstairs, collected the shopping list from Mrs. Bird and his basket on wheels, and disappeared out of the house with a purposeful gleam in his eyes.

Pausing only to call in at the bakers, where he had a standing order for freshly baked buns, Paddington soon rounded the corner into the Portobello Road and made his way in the direction of Mr. Gruber's shop with its familiar windows bursting at the seams with antiques of every shape and size.

Mr. Gruber shared Paddington's liking for cocoa and buns, and they often had long chats together over their elevenses. He had travelled a great deal in his younger days and Paddington felt sure he would know all there was to know about holidays abroad.

Mr. Gruber was as excited as Paddington when he

heard the news and he quickly led the way to the horsehair sofa at the back of the shop which he reserved for all their more important discussions.

"What a nice surprise, Mr. Brown," he said, as he busied himself at the stove with a saucepan of milk. "I don't suppose there are many bears able to take their holidays abroad, so you must make the most of it. If there's anything I can do to help, you must let me know."

Mr. Gruber listened carefully to all Paddington's explanations while he made the cocoa and his face took on a serious expression.

" I must say being in charge of an itinerary sounds a heavy responsibility for a young bear's shoulders, Mr. Brown," he exclaimed as he handed Paddington a steaming mug of cocoa in exchange for a bun. " I shall have to see what I can do."

And without further ado he got down on his hands and knees and began sorting through a pile of old books in a box behind the sofa.

" Everyone seems to be taking their holidays abroad at the moment, Mr. Brown," he said, as he began handing some of the books up to Paddington. " I've had rather a run on books about France, but I hope you'll find these useful."

Paddington's eyes got larger and larger as the pile by his side got higher, and he nearly fell off his seat with surprise when Mr. Gruber suddenly stood up holding an old black beret in his hands.

" It's rather large," said Mr. Gruber apologetically, as he held it up to the light, " and there seem to be one or two moth holes. But it's a real French one and you're very welcome to use it."

" Thank you very much, Mr. Gruber," said Paddington gratefully. " I expect the moth holes will do for my ears. Bears' ears don't fold very easily."

"Well, I hope you find everything useful," said Mr. Gruber, looking very pleased at the expression on Paddington's face. "You'll need a lot of books if you're going to plan an itinerary and it's as well to be on the safe side. You never know what might happen when you're abroad, Mr. Brown."

Mr. Gruber went on to explain about some of the things Paddington would see while he was away, and it was some while before Paddington wiped the last of the cocoa stains from his whiskers and stood up to go. Time passed very quickly when he was with Mr. Gruber because he always made things sound so much more interesting than other people did.

"I expect you'll find lots to write in your scrap-book, Mr. Brown," said Mr. Gruber as he helped Paddington load his shopping basket. "I shall look forward to reading all about it."

Paddington felt more and more excited as he waved good-bye and staggered along the Portobello Road under the weight of all his belongings. The shopping basket was so heavy it was quite difficult to steer, and several times he nearly ran into one or other of the barrows which lined the street.

Apart from that there were so many things on his mind he didn't know which to think about first. He was particularly anxious to try out his new beret, and some of Mr. Gruber's books looked most interesting. In the end he decided to sit down for a rest and investigate both.

He put his old hat on the ground, carefully adjusted the beret, and then began taking the books out of his shopping basket one by one.

First there was a dictionary. Then there was a French cookery book—full of recipes and coloured pictures of food which made his mouth water. After that came one packed with maps and instructions about things to see and do, and this was followed by several more books full of pictures.

Last of all Paddington came to a very important-looking leather-bound volume which had the words " Useful Phrases for the Traveller Abroad " written in gold letters on its cover.

Before he took it out of the basket Paddington hurried across the road and dipped his paws in a nearby horse-trough. Mr. Gruber had explained that the book was very old and he'd asked him to take especial care of it.

When he returned Paddington sat down again and began to examine the book. It was most unusual and he didn't remember ever having seen one quite like it before. Just inside the front cover there was a drawing which showed what looked like a very old-fashioned car being drawn by four white horses, and it was full of sentences showing how to ask for things in French, with pictures explaining matters as it went along.

In no time at all he became so lost in the book he quite forgot where he was. There was one particularly interesting phrase in a section marked " Trayel " which caught his eye at once. It said " My Grandmother has fallen out of the Stage-coach and needs attention."

Paddington felt sure it would come in very useful if Mrs. Bird happened to fall out of Mr. Brown's car while they were going along and he tested it several times, waving his paws in the air as the man in the picture seemed to be doing.

To his surprise, when he looked up, Paddington discovered he was surrounded by a small crowd of people who were watching him with interest.

" If you arsks me," said one man, who was leaning on a bicycle studying Paddington intently, " I reckon he's one of them onion bears. They come over every year from Brittany," he added knowledgeably as he turned to the crowd. " They 'as their onions on a piece of string. You must 'ave seen 'em. That's why 'e was spouting French."

" Garn," said another man. " That wasn't French. He was 'aving some sort of spasm. Waving 'is paws about something shocking 'e was. Besides," he added triumphantly, " if he's an onion bear where's his onions ? "

" Perhaps he's lost them," said someone else. " That's why he's upset. I expect his string broke if the truth be known."

" It's enough to give anyone a spasm," said a lady, " coming all this way and then losing your onions."

" That's what I said," exclaimed the first man.
" I expect he was 'aving a French spasm. They're
the worst of the lot. Very excitable, them foreigners."

" I shouldn't touch him, dear," said another lady,

turning to her small boy who had his eye on Paddington's beret. " You don't know where he's been."

Paddington's eyes had been getting larger and
larger as he listened to the crowd and he looked most
offended at the last remark.

" An onion bear! " he exclaimed at last. " I'm not

19

an onion bear. I'm a going abroad bear and I've just been to see Mr. Gruber!"

With that he gathered up his belongings and hurried off up the road, leaving behind him a buzz of conversation.

Rounding the corner into Windsor Gardens, Paddington gave the crowd several hard stares over his shoulder, but as he got nearer to the familiar green front door of No. 32 a thoughtful expression came over his face.

And as he stood on the doorstep and heard the footsteps of Mrs. Bird coming along the hall Paddington decided that perhaps it had been a very good morning's work after all.

Thinking things over he felt rather pleased at having been mistaken for a French bear—even if it had only been one who sold onions. In fact the more he thought about the matter the better pleased he became, and he felt sure that with the help of all the maps and pamphlets and Mr. Gruber's books he would be able to plan some very good holiday " doings " indeed for the Browns.

CHAPTER TWO

A Visit to the Bank

" PADDINGTON LOOKS unusually smart this morning," said Mrs. Bird.

" Oh, dear," said Mrs. Brown. " Does he? I hope he's not up to anything."

She joined Mrs. Bird at the window and followed the direction of her gaze up the road to where a small figure in a blue duffle coat was hurrying along the pavement.

Now that Mrs. Bird mentioned it Paddington did

seem to have an air about him. Even from a distance
his fur looked remarkably neat and freshly combed,
and his old hat, instead of being pulled down over his
ears, was set at a very rakish angle with the brim
turned up, which was most unusual. Even his old
suitcase looked as if it had had some kind of polish
on it.

" He's not even going in his usual direction," said
Mrs. Brown as Paddington, having reached the end
of the road, looked carefully over his shoulder and
then turned right and quickly disappeared from view.
" He *always* turns left."

" If you ask me," said Mrs. Bird, " that young
bear's got something on his mind. He was acting
strangely at breakfast this morning. He didn't even
have a second helping and he kept peering over Mr.
Brown's shoulder at the paper with a very odd look
on his face."

" I'm not surprised he had an odd look if it was
Henry's paper," said Mrs. Brown. " I can never
make head or tail of it myself."

Mr. Brown worked in the City of London and he
always read a very important newspaper at breakfast
time, full of news about stocks and shares and other
money matters, which the rest of the Browns found
very dull.

" All the same," she continued, as she led the way
into the kitchen, " it's very strange. I do hope he

hasn't got one of his ideas coming on. He spent most of yesterday evening doing his accounts and that's often a bad sign."

Mrs. Brown and Mrs. Bird were hard at work preparing for the coming holiday, and with only a few days left there were a thousand and one things to be done. If they hadn't been quite so busy they might well have put two and two together, but as it was the matter of Paddington's strange behaviour was soon forgotten in the rush to get everything ready.

Unaware of the interest he had caused, Paddington made his way along a road not far from the Portobello market until he reached an imposing building which stood slightly apart from the rest. It had tall, bronze doors which were tightly shut, and over the entrance, in large gold letters, were the words FLOYDS BANK LIMITED.

After carefully making sure that no one was watching, Paddington withdrew a small cardboard-covered book from under his hat and then sat down on his suitcase outside the bank while he waited for the doors to open.

Like the building the book had the words FLOYDS BANK printed on the outside, and just inside the front cover it had P. BROWN ESQ., written in ink.

With the exception of the Browns and Mr. Gruber not many people knew about Paddington's banking account as it was a closely kept secret. It had all started some months before when Paddington came across an advertisement in one of Mr. Brown's old newspapers which he cut out and saved. In it a very fatherly-looking man smoking a pipe, who said he was a Mr. Floyd, explained how any money left with him would earn what he called " interest," and that the longer he kept it the more it would be worth.

Paddington had an eye for a bargain and having his money increase simply by leaving it somewhere had sounded like a very good bargain indeed.

The Browns had been so pleased at the idea that Mr. Brown had given him three shillings to add to his Christmas and birthday money, and after a great deal of thought Paddington had himself added another sixpence which he'd carefully saved from his weekly bun allowance. When all these sums were added together they made a grand total of one pound, three shillings and sixpence, and one day Mrs. Bird had taken him along to the bank in order to open an account.

For several days afterwards Paddington had hung about in a shop doorway opposite casting suspicious glances at anyone who went in or out. But after having been moved on by a passing policeman he'd had to let matters rest.

Since then, although he had carefully checked the amount in his book several times, Paddington had never actually been inside the bank. Secretly he was rather overawed by all the marble and thick polished wood, so he was pleased when at long last ten o'clock began to strike on a nearby church clock and he was still the only one outside.

As the last of the chimes died away there came the sound of bolts being withdrawn on the other side of the door, and Paddington hurried forward to peer eagerly through the letter-box.

" 'Ere, 'ere," exclaimed the porter, as he caught sight of Paddington's hat through the slit. " No hawkers 'ere, young feller-me-lad. This is a bank— not a workhouse. We don't want no hobbledehoys hanging around here."

" Hobbledehoys? " repeated Paddington, letting go of the letter-box flap in his surprise.

" That's what I said," grumbled the porter as he opened the door. " Breathing all over me knockers. I 'as to polish that brass, yer know."

" I'm not a hobbledehoy," exclaimed Paddington, looking most offended as he waved his bank book in the air. " I'm a bear and I've come to see Mr. Floyd about my savings."

" Ho, dear," said the porter, taking a closer look at Paddington. " Beggin' yer pardon, sir. When I saw your whiskers poking through me letter-box I mistook you for one of them bearded gentlemen of the road."

" That's all right," said Paddington sadly. " I often

get mistaken." And as the man held the door open for him he raised his hat politely and hurried into the bank.

On several occasions in the past Mrs. Bird had

impressed on Paddington how wise it was to have money in the bank in case of a rainy day and how he might be glad of it one day for a special occasion. Thinking things over in bed the night before, Paddington had decided that going abroad for a holiday was very much a special occasion, and after studying the advertisement once again he had thought up a very good idea for having the best of both worlds, but like many ideas he had at night under the bedclothes it didn't seem quite such a good one in the cold light of day.

Now that he was actually inside the bank, Paddington began to feel rather guilty and he wished he'd consulted Mr. Gruber on the matter, for he wasn't at all sure that Mrs. Bird would approve of his taking any money out without first asking her.

Hurrying across to one of the cubby-holes in the counter, Padddington climbed up on his suitcase and peered over the edge. The man on the other side looked rather startled when Paddington's hat appeared over the top and he reached nervously for a nearby ink-well.

" I'd like to take out all my savings for a special occasion, please," said Paddington importantly, as he handed the man his book.

Looking rather relieved, the man took Paddington's book from him and then raised one eyebrow as he held it up to the light. There were a number of calculations in red ink all over the cover, not to mention blots and one or two rather messy-looking marmalade stains.

" I'm afraid I had an accident with one of my jars under the bedclothes last night," explained Paddington hastily as he caught the man's eye.

" One of your *jars*? " repeated the man. " Under the *bedclothes*? "

" That's right," said Paddington. " I was working out my interest and I stepped back into it by mistake. It's a bit difficult under the bedclothes."

" It must be," said the man distastefully. " Marmalade stains indeed! And on a Floyds bank book! "

He hadn't been with the branch for very long, and although the manager had told him they sometimes had some very odd customers to deal with nothing had been mentioned about bears' banking accounts.

" What would you like me to do with it? " he asked doubtfully.

" I'd like to leave all my interest in, please," explained Paddington. " In case it rains."

" Well," said the man in a superior tone of voice as he made some calculations on a piece of paper. " I'm afraid you won't keep very dry on this. It only comes to threepence."

" *What*! " exclaimed Paddington, hardly able to believe his ears. " *Threepence*! I don't think that's very interesting."

"Interest isn't the same thing as interesting," said the man. "Not the same thing at all."

He tried hard to think of some way of explaining matters for he wasn't used to dealing with bears and he had a feeling that Paddington was going to be one of his more difficult customers.

"It's . . . it's something we give you for letting us borrow your money," he said. "The longer you leave it in the more you get."

"Well, my money's been in since just after Christmas," exclaimed Paddington. "That's nearly six months."

"Threepence," said the man firmly.

Paddington watched in a daze as the man made an entry in his book and then pushed a one-pound note and some silver across the counter. "There you are," he said briskly. "One pound, three shillings and sixpence."

Paddington looked suspiciously at the note and then consulted a piece of paper he held in his paw. His eyes grew larger and larger as he compared the two.

"I think you must have made a mistake," he exclaimed. "This isn't my note."

"A mistake?" said the man stiffly. "We of Floyds never make mistakes."

"But it's got a different number," said Paddington hotly.

29

" A *different number*? " repeated the man.

" Yes," said Paddington. " And it said on mine that you promised to pay bear one pound on demand."

" Not *bear*," said the assistant. " Bear*er*. It says that on all notes. Besides," he continued, " you don't get the same note back that you put in. I expect yours is miles away by now if it's anywhere at all. It might even have been burnt if it was an old one. They often burn old notes when they're worn out."

" *Burnt*? " repeated Paddington in a dazed voice. " *You've burnt my note*? "

" I didn't say it *had* been," said the man, looking more and more confused. " I only said it might have been."

Paddington took a deep breath and gave the assistant a hard stare. It was one of the extra special hard ones which his Aunt Lucy had taught him and which he kept for emergencies.

" I think I should like to see Mr. Floyd," he exclaimed.

" Mr. Floyd? " repeated the assistant. He mopped his brow nervously as he looked anxiously over Paddington's shoulder at the queue which was already beginning to form. There were some nasty murmurings going on at the back which he didn't like the sound of at all. " I'm afraid there isn't a Mr. Floyd," he said.

" We have a Mr. Trimble," he added hastily, as

Paddington gave him an even harder stare. " He's the manager. I think perhaps I'd better fetch him —he'll know what to do."

Paddington stared indignantly after the retreating figure of the clerk as he made his way towards a door marked MANAGER. The more he saw of things the less he liked the look of them. Not only did his note have a different number but he had just caught sight of the dates on the coins and they were quite different to those on the ones he had left. Apart from that his own coins had been highly polished, whereas these were old and very dull.

Paddington climbed down off his suitcase and pushed his way through the crowd with a determined expression on his face. Although he was only small, Paddington was a bear with a strong sense of right and wrong, especially when it came to money matters, and he felt it was high time he took matters into his own paws.

After he had made his way out of the bank Paddington hurried down the road in the direction of a red kiosk. Locked away in the secret compartment of his suitcase there was a note with some special instructions Mrs. Bird had written out for him in case of an emergency, together with four pennies. Thinking things over as he went along, Paddington decided it was very much a matter of an emergency, in fact he had a job to remember when he'd had a bigger one, and he was glad when at long last the telephone kiosk came into view and he saw it was empty.

" I don't know what's going on at the bank this morning," said Mrs. Brown as she closed the front door. " There was an enormous crowd outside when I came past."

" Perhaps there's been a robbery," said Mrs. Bird. " You read of such nasty goings on these days."

" I don't think it was a robbery," said Mrs. Brown vaguely. " It was more like an emergency of some kind. The police were there and an ambulance *and* the fire-brigade."

" H'mm! " said Mrs. Bird. " Well, I hope for all our sakes it isn't anything serious. Paddington's got all his money there and if there has been a raid we shall never hear the last of it."

Mrs. Bird paused as she was speaking and a thoughtful expression came over her face. " Talking of Paddington, have you seen him since he went out? " she asked.

" No," said Mrs. Brown. " Good heavens! " she exclaimed. " You don't think . . ."

" I'll get my hat," said Mrs. Bird. " And if Paddington's not somewhere at the bottom of it all I'll eat it on the way home! "

It took Mrs. Brown and Mrs. Bird some while to force their way through the crowd into the bank, and when they at last got inside their worst suspicions were realised, for there, sitting on his suitcase in the middle of a large crowd of officials was the small figure of Paddington.

" What on earth's going on? " cried Mrs. Brown, as they pushed their way through to the front.

Paddington looked very thankful to see the others. Things had been going from bad to worse since he'd got back to the bank.

" I think my numbers have got mixed up by mistake, Mrs. Brown," he explained.

" Trying to do a young bear out of his life's savings, that's what's going on," cried someone at the back.

" Set fire to his notes, they did," cried someone else.

" 'Undreds of pounds gone up in smoke, so they say," called out a street trader who knew Paddington by sight and had come into the bank to see what all the fuss was about.

" Oh, dear," said Mrs. Brown nervously. " I'm sure there must be some mistake. I don't think Floyds would ever do a thing like that on purpose."

" Indeed not, madam," exclaimed the manager as he stepped forward.

" My name's Trimble," he continued. " Can you vouch for this young bear? "

" Vouch for him? " said Mrs. Bird. " Why, I brought him here myself in the first place. He's a

most respectable member of the family and very law-abiding."

"Respectable he may be," said a large policeman, as he licked his pencil, "but I don't know so much about being law-abiding. Dialling 999 he was without proper cause. Calling out the police, not to mention the fire-brigade and an ambulance. It'll all have to be gone into in the proper manner."

Everyone stopped talking and looked down at Paddington.

"I was only trying to ring Mrs. Bird," said Paddington.

"Trying to ring Mrs. Bird?" repeated the policeman slowly, as he wrote it down in his notebook.

"That's right," explained Paddington. "I'm afraid I got my paw stuck in number nine, and every time I tried to get it out someone asked me what I wanted so I shouted for help."

Mr. Trimble coughed. "I think perhaps we had better go into my office," he said. "It all sounds most complicated and it's much quieter in there."

With that everyone agreed wholeheartedly. And Paddington, as he picked up his suitcase and followed the others into the manager's office, agreed most of all. Having a banking account was quite the most complicated thing he had ever come across.

It was some while before Paddington finally got through his explanations, but when he had finished everyone looked most relieved that the matter wasn't more serious. Even the policeman seemed quite pleased.

" It's a pity there aren't more public-spirited bears about," he said, shaking Paddington by the paw. " If everyone called for help when they saw anything suspicious we'd have a lot less work to do in the long run."

After everyone else had left, Mr. Trimble took Mrs. Brown, Mrs. Bird and Paddington on a tour of the strong-room to show them where all the money was kept, and he even gave Paddington a book of instructions so that he would know exactly what to do the next time he paid the bank a visit.

" I do hope you *won't* close your account, Mr. Brown," he said. " We of Floyds never like to feel we're losing a valued customer. If you like to leave your three and sixpence with us for safe keeping I'll let you have a brand-new one-pound note to take away for your holidays."

Paddington thanked Mr. Trimble very much for all his trouble and then considered the matter. " If you don't mind," he said at last, " I think I'd like a used one instead."

Paddington wasn't the sort of bear who believed in taking any chances, and although the crisp new note in the manager's hand looked very tempting he decided he would much prefer to have one that had been properly tested.

CHAPTER THREE

Trouble at the Airport

EXCITEMENT MOUNTED in the Browns' house during the few days that were left before the holiday. Paddington in particular was kept very busy, and he made a large number of trips between Windsor Gardens and the Portobello Road in order to consult Mr. Gruber on the various problems which came up.

They had quite a number of chats sitting together in their deck-chairs on the pavement in front of the shop and Mr. Gruber had to get in an extra supply of cocoa to help out.

The Browns began saying "excuse me" to one another in French whenever they met, and Mrs. Bird spent several evenings making a special label for Paddington to tie round his neck. It was a large label bound with best quality leather and it had the Browns' address printed on it together with the words "Finder will be rewarded" in several languages. Mrs. Bird viewed the idea of going abroad with great suspicion and she didn't want to run any risks.

But at long last the great day arrived and No. 32 Windsor Gardens was ablaze with light from a very early hour.

Paddington was the first up for he had a lot of last-minute packing to do. He had collected a great many things during his travels and he didn't want to leave any of them behind in case of burglars.

Apart from his old hat—which he was wearing, and his suitcase—which he would be carrying, there was his duffle coat, a bucket and spade—which he had kept clean and highly polished ever since his last visit to the seaside, a disguise outfit, a magic set, a large jar of marmalade in case of emergencies—Mr. Gruber had explained that it might be difficult to get the kind of marmalade he liked in France—the itinerary and other important papers, not to mention his leather-bound scrapbook, some ink and glue, and all the books Mr. Gruber had given him, together with a Union

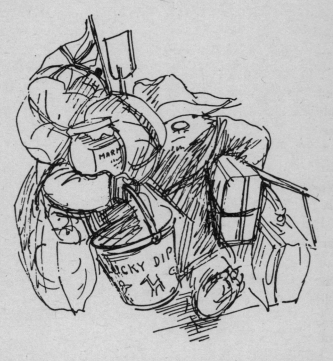

Jack on a stick and an old tea towel of Mrs. Bird's which had a map of France printed on it and which he had rescued from the dustbin some days before.

Soon the rest of the household was wakened by the noise as Paddington hurried about his room doing up parcels, and shortly afterwards the sound of frying bacon and the tinkle of breakfast plates added itself to the general hubbub.

"Goodness gracious!" exclaimed Mrs. Bird, as

she went upstairs to call the others for breakfast and met a large assortment of parcels coming the other way. " Whatever's going on?"

" It's all right, Mrs. Bird," gasped Paddington, from behind a particularly large carrier bag. " It's only me. I think I've got my magic wand stuck in the banisters."

" Your magic wand?" echoed Mr. Brown, as he started to come down the stairs. " Good heavens! We're only going on holiday—we're not going to *live* in France!"

Paddington looked crestfallenly at the pile of parcels as the others disentangled his wand from the banisters and helped him down the stairs. Now that Mr. Brown mentioned it there did seem to be rather a lot of things.

" Perhaps I could lock some of them in the cupboard under the stairs," he said, amid general agreement.

But even with several of Paddington's parcels gone, by the time Mr. Brown had finished loading the car with suitcases and beach balls, a tent, fishing-rods, and a thousand and one other things it didn't seem possible they would get to the end of Windsor Gardens let alone reach France.

" I thought the idea of a holiday was to have a good rest," gasped Mrs. Bird as she was wedged into the back seat alongside Jonathan and Judy. " I'm worn out already."

" It's all right, Mrs. Bird," exclaimed Paddington

importantly from the front seat as he consulted his ' doings list.' " We stop for a snack soon."

" We stop for a snack? " echoed Mr. Brown. " But we haven't even started yet! "

Mrs. Brown sighed as she removed Paddington's Union Jack from her left ear. She was quite sure other families didn't have so much bother when they went on holiday.

But for all the grumbling it was a happy party of Browns who shortly afterwards sailed through the streets of London on their way to the coast.

Soon they were speeding through the hop-fields and orchards of Kent, and it seemed no time at all before Mr. Brown turned off the main road and drove into the airport.

It was the first time Paddington had ever visited an airport, and although he had often seen and heard aeroplanes in the sky he had never given them much thought before. As Mr. Brown brought the car to a stop and they all climbed out he looked around excitedly at all the planes standing on the runways waiting to take off.

From where he was standing they looked much smaller than he had expected. Even through his opera-glasses they weren't a great deal bigger, and when he heard that not only were they all about to go up in one but that Mr. Brown's car was going as well, a thought-ful expression came over his face.

" Come along everyone," called Mr. Brown briskly,

as he led the way towards the airport buildings. " We haven't much time."

The Browns trooped in through the entrance door and followed Mr. Brown across the hall to a desk marked RECEPTION.

" A party of Browns for the Continent," said Mr. Brown, as he handed the girl behind the desk a pile of tickets.

" This way, please," said the girl, leading the way down a corridor and through yet another door marked IMMIGRATION, to where a man in a dark blue suit was standing.

" Have your passports ready, please."

As the girl spoke Mrs. Bird stopped suddenly in her tracks and clutched Mrs. Brown's arm. " Mercy me! " she exclaimed.

" Whatever's the matter, Mrs. Bird? " asked Mrs. Brown, looking most concerned. " You've gone quite pale."

" Passports! " exclaimed Mrs. Bird. " What about Paddington's passport? "

" *Paddington's?* " echoed Mrs. Brown, turning pale herself.

The Browns looked at each other in alarm. In the general excitement of planning the holiday and filling in all the forms no one had even given a thought to the idea of Paddington needing a passport.

" Do bears have them? " asked Mr. Brown vaguely. " After all, he's got a label."

"I don't know about their *having* them," replied Mrs. Bird ominously. "The question is, knowing Paddington, will they give him one? After all, think of his circumstances!"

The others fell silent as the full meaning of Mrs. Bird's remarks sank in, for Paddington's circumstances *were* a trifle unusual to say the least. He had travelled by himself to England all the way from Peru as a stowaway in a lifeboat, and although he hadn't taken up much room and had used his own marmalade, the Browns were quite sure that the owners of the boat, not to mention the customs men and all kinds of other officials, would be most upset if they ever found out.

As if in answer to their thoughts, the man in the dark blue suit grew very stern as he listened to their conversation. "What's all this?" he exclaimed. "Did I hear you say there's someone here without a passport? I'm afraid we can't have that sort of thing, you know. You can't go abroad without a passport —it's against the regulations. Ask him to step forward."

"Oh, dear," groaned Judy as the Browns looked round, only to discover that Paddington was nowhere in sight. "Wherever has he got to now?"

"Crikey!" said Jonathan. "Trust old Paddington to disappear when he's most wanted."

"What's his name?" asked the official, taking a piece of paper and a pen.

44

" Well," said Mr. Brown, " it's Brown—Padding-ton Brown—in a way . . ."

" In a *way*? " repeated the man suspiciously. " In *what* way? "

" We called him that when we found him on Paddington Station," began Mrs. Brown. " He's a bear and he comes from Darkest Peru and . . ." Her voice trailed away as she caught sight of the expression on the immigration man's face.

" A bear without a passport," clucked the man. " And travelling under a false name. This is a serious matter."

But before he had time to go on and tell the Browns just how serious a matter it was the door at the far end of the corridor burst open and Paddington hurried through with an anxious expression on his face and a red-faced commissionaire hard on his paws.

" I found 'im," said the commissionaire, breathing heavily, " looking at some aeroplanes through these 'ere h'opera-glasses. And what's more," he added sternly, handing Paddington's notebook to the im-migration man, " 'e was writing down notes in this 'ere book."

" That's my scrapbook," exclaimed Paddington, looking most upset.

" H'mm! " said the commissionaire. " I don't know about that. There's some funny-looking scraps if you ask me. Don't know as I like the look of some of them at all."

" Carrying a disguise outfit wrapped up in brown paper he was too! " he continued, placing a parcel on the counter.

" Oh, dear," groaned Mrs. Brown. " I knew he should have left it at home."

" If you asks me," said the commissionaire, " 'e was up to no good. 'Ighly suspicious it was."

" Well, bear," said the immigration man. " What have you to say? "

Paddington took a deep breath and raised his hat. " I was only making notes for Mr. Gruber," he began.

There was a nasty silence as something white and sticky landed with a plop on the floor. The commissionaire picked it up between thumb and forefinger and stared at it.

" It seems to be some kind of marmalade sandwich," said the immigration man doubtfully, as he looked up at the ceiling.

" It *is* a marmalade sandwich," explained Paddington. " I expect it fell out of my hat. I usually keep one under there when I go out in case of an emergency."

" I've never heard of anyone smuggling marmalade sandwiches before," said the man. " I think this is a matter for the customs."

" And that's not all," said the commissionaire, as he placed Paddington's suitcase on the counter and gave it a smart rap with his knuckles. " There's

something funny about this 'ere. It's a lot thicker on the outside for what there is inside—if you see what I mean."

"Looking at aeroplanes through opera-glasses," said the immigration man sternly, as he reached down and picked up a telephone. "Carrying a disguise outfit. Smuggling marmalade sandwiches . . . all this will have to be gone into."

"Perhaps he's one of them international bears," said the commissionaire hopefully. "Probably got stuff hidden in his fur. I don't suppose that's real marmalade in them sandwiches if the truth be known."

"We shall have to examine the shreds very carefully," said the immigration man as he replaced the telephone.

Paddington looked at the man as if he could hardly believe his ears. "Examine my *shreds!*" he exclaimed hotly. "That's some of my special marmalade from the cut-price grocer!"

Paddington gave the man a number of hard stares from under his hat. The immigration man began fingering his collar nervously and he looked very relieved when a door opened behind him and an even more important-looking official came into the room.

"That's him," said the immigration man, pointing at Paddington. "The short, furry one with the hat."

"There's something funny with his circs," said the commissionaire.

"My *circs!*" exclaimed Paddington, looking more and more alarmed. "But I felt all right at breakfast this morning."

"He means your circumstances, dear," said Mrs. Brown, glaring at the commissionaire.

"Now, look here . . ." began Mr. Brown.

"I'm sorry, sir," said the second official firmly. "I'm afraid I must ask you to wait here while we question the young, er . . . gentleman." He motioned the Browns to one side as he lifted up a flap in the counter and led the way towards his office.

Paddington looked most upset as he picked up his

suitcase and parcel and followed the man. " Oh, dear," he said, as he looked forlornly over his shoulder at the others, " I hope my circumstances *are* all right! "

" Poor old Paddington," said Jonathan as the door closed behind him.

" He does look a bit suspicious sometimes," said Judy. " Especially if you don't know him."

Mrs. Bird gripped her umbrella firmly. " If that bear *is* in trouble," she exclaimed, " they'll have me to deal with—and I don't care who I have to go and see about it."

" I hope they *don't* find the secret compartment in his suitcase," said Judy. " It won't look too good if they do."

" I bet they don't," said Jonathan. " No one's ever seen inside Paddington's secret compartment. It's a jolly good one."

" It's all your fault, Henry," said Mrs. Brown, turning to her husband. " It was your idea to go abroad for a holiday."

" I like that! " said Mr. Brown indignantly. " Everyone else was keen enough at the time."

But even Mr. Brown began to look more and more serious as the minutes ticked by and there was still no sign of Paddington.

" You don't think," said Mrs. Brown, voicing the thoughts of them all, " you don't think they'd send him back to Peru, do you? "

" Just let them try," said Mrs. Bird, glaring at the closed door. " Just let them try! "

But by the time the door did finally open and the head official beckoned them in, the Browns, as they trooped into the office, were prepared for the worst.

" Well," said Mr. Brown, as he settled back in his aeroplane seat and fastened the safety belt, " all's well that ends well. But I didn't think half an hour ago we should all be sitting here. Fancy Paddington having a passport all the time."

" It was in the secret compartment in my suitcase, Mr. Brown," said Paddington. " With all my other important papers."

" Well," said Mrs. Bird, " I must say I didn't really think Paddington's Aunt Lucy would have let him come all this way without one. From all I've heard, she sounds a very wise old bear and it would have been most unlike her.

" Anyway," she added, " it's a great load off my mind to know that young bear's circumstances *are* all right."

" But what I can't understand, Paddington," said Mr. Brown, " is why you didn't say you had it in the first place. It would have saved an awful lot of bother."

Paddington put on one of his injured expressions. " No one asked me, Mr. Brown," he said. " I thought it was my circumstances."

Mr. Brown coughed and the others exchanged

glances. Fortunately at that moment there was a loud roar from the engines and as the plane started to move along the runway the subject was hurriedly forgotten in the general excitement.

"Now we can all look forward to a nice holiday abroad with no worries," said Mrs. Bird a few minutes later, as the plane levelled out and she began to undo her safety belt.

And to that the Browns, as they looked out of the cabin windows at the blue sea glinting in the sunlight far below, echoed a heartfelt "Hear! Hear!"

Paddington was the only one who didn't join in for he was much too busy consulting his "doings list." He had just discovered that in the excitement at the airport they had forgotten to have lunch. But he was pleased to see that on the very next page there was an entry which said:

ARRIVE IN FRANCE—SNAK

"And a very good idea, too," said Mr. Brown approvingly, when Paddington showed it to him. "There's nothing like a spot of excitement over a young bear's circumstances to make you hungry."

CHAPTER FOUR

Paddington Saves the Day

" You wouldn't think," said Mrs. Brown, looking hard at her husband, " that it would be possible to get lost in such a short space of time. We've only been in France half a day."

" Are you sure you don't know where we are, Paddington? " asked Mr. Brown for the umpteenth time.

Paddington shook his head sadly. " I think we must have taken the wrong turning by mistake, Mr. Brown," he admitted.

The Browns looked gloomily at one another. Until that moment their first day in France had been very gay and exciting. With so many new things to see, the time had passed very quickly and Paddington in particular had been kept busy following the route with his paw and making notes as they went along.

On the journey along the coast they had passed through a number of towns and he'd been most impressed by the sight of all the bustling traffic on the wrong side of the road and the people sitting at tables on the pavement outside cafés.

Between the towns they had driven along miles of straight country roads lined on either side by tall poplar trees and past tiny villages full of men in blue overalls and women hurrying to and fro carrying long loaves of bread.

Nicest of all, every now and then as they turned a corner, they'd had a glimpse of the blue sea and heard the distant roar of waves breaking on the shore.

And then, as they crossed into Brittany, not only had the countryside gradually become much wilder, but things had started to go wrong as well.

First the wide black road had suddenly changed into a narrow lane covered in stones. Then the lane had become a cart-track. Finally the cart-track had come to an end on a piece of common land, and as a final blow the car had punctured one of its back tyres.

Being in charge of the itinerary, Paddington felt very upset at what had happened and he peered hard at the maps while the Browns gathered anxiously round him.

" What was the name of the last place we went through, Paddington? " asked Mr. Brown. " Perhaps that's where we went wrong."

" I think it was called *Gravillons*, Mr. Brown," said Paddington. " But I can't see it on any of the maps."

" *Gravillons*," repeated Mr. Brown. " That's funny. I seem to remember seeing that written up somewhere too. Are you sure you can't find it? " He bent over and looked at the map while Paddington examined Mrs. Bird's old tea towel hopefully.

" Crikey! " exclaimed Jonathan suddenly, as he looked up from his dictionary. " No wonder you can't find it on the map. *Gravillons* isn't a place—it's a road sign—it means ' loose chippings '! "

" *What*! " exclaimed Paddington hotly. " *Loose chippings*! "

" That's where all those stones were," said Judy. " They must have been repairing the road."

Mrs. Bird snorted. " *Gravillons* indeed! " she exclaimed. " No wonder that poor bear went wrong. It's a mercy we didn't all end up in the sea." Mrs. Bird firmly believed that everything abroad should be written in good, plain English.

" Oh, well," said Mr. Brown, as he folded the

map. " At least we know where we're *not*, even if we don't know where we are."

He looked down at the pile of luggage which hid the spare wheel in the boot of the car. " Everything will have to come out so I vote we make the best of it and have a picnic while I change the wheel."

Mrs. Brown and Mrs. Bird, who had been looking forward to having a rest and a nice meal in a comfortable hotel, didn't look very pleased at the idea, but Jonathan, Judy and Paddington were most excited. Paddington in particular thought it was a very good idea of Mr. Brown's. He liked picnics and it was a long time since he'd had one.

" It's a good thing I brought some food along," said Mrs. Bird, as she opened her travelling bag and began to take out an assortment of tins and packets together with a loaf of bread and some knives and forks. " I had a feeling we might need it."

" I tell you what," said Mr. Brown. " We'll have a competition. You can each cook one of the courses and I'll give a prize for the best one."

Mr. Brown was very keen on competitions. He had a vague idea that it kept people out of mischief.

" Wizzo! " exclaimed Jonathan. " Bags we have a camp-fire."

" I'll collect some firewood if you like, Mr. Brown," said Paddington, waving his paw in the direction of a wood at the top of a nearby hill. " Bears are good at collecting firewood."

"Don't go too far," called Mrs. Brown anxiously, as Paddington picked up his suitcase and hurried off. "We don't want you getting lost as well."

But Paddington was already out of earshot. He was still feeling guilty that the Browns had lost their way and he was anxious to make amends by gathering as much firewood as possible, so he hurried up the hill as fast as his legs would carry him.

But looking around and sniffing the air as he made his way across the springy turf, Paddington decided that perhaps being lost wasn't quite such a bad thing after all.

To start with there was a nice, warm smell about everything which he liked very much indeed. It was an interesting smell—not at all like the one in England, or even in Peru for that matter. It seemed to be made up of coffee and newly baked bread as well as several other things he couldn't quite place, and for some strange reason it was getting stronger every minute.

It wasn't until Paddington reached the top of the hill and looked down over the other side that he discovered the reason for it, and when he did so he had to rub his eyes several times in order to make sure he wasn't dreaming.

For there, only a short distance away at the bottom of the hill and looking exactly like one of the pictures in Mr. Brown's pamphlets, was a cluster of houses, and beyond the houses he could see a beach and a small harbour full of boats.

Running up from the harbour there was a narrow street which led into a square where there were a number of gaily-coloured stalls laden with fruit and vegetables.

Paddington waved his paws wildly in the Browns' direction and called out several times but they were much too far away for him to make them hear, and so he took out his opera-glasses and sat down for a moment to consider the matter.

As he peered through his glasses at the village a thoughtful expression gradually came over his face, and when he stood up again a few minutes later there was an excited gleam in his eyes as well. Apart from the fact that it was all very strange and definitely needed investigating, Paddington had an idea starting in the back of his mind and the more he thought about it the more anxious he became to test it out.

As he hurried down the hill into the village and made his way towards the square which he'd seen from the top of the hill, Paddington looked around with interest. He liked new places and this one seemed particularly nice.

On his right there was a large building with a veranda and a sign outside which said *Hôtel du Centre*, and on the other side of the square there was a Post Office and a butcher's shop as well as several cafés and a grocery store.

Best of all, next door to the hotel he spied a baker's shop. Paddington liked baker's shops and this one

was most interesting, for it had loaves of every shape
and size in its window—long ones, short ones, fat
ones, round ones—in fact, he grew quite dizzy trying
to count them all.

After consulting Mr. Gruber's phrase-book, Paddington made his way across the square in the direction
of the shop. In the past he had often found bakers
were most understanding as far as bears' problems

were concerned—Mr. Gruber always said it was something to do with their sharing an interest in buns —but whatever the reason, Paddington decided he couldn't do better than pay the owner a visit and seek his advice about the surprise he had in mind for the Browns.

" Paddington's being very mysterious all of a sudden," said Mr. Brown, some while later.

" If you ask me," said Mrs. Bird, " that bear's got something up his paw. He was gone a very long time when he went for the firewood and he's had a funny look on his face ever since."

The Browns were in the middle of their meal and there was a slight hold-up while Paddington prepared his contribution.

Jonathan and Judy had already made some soup in Mr. Brown's billy-can, and Mrs. Bird had followed that with a special salad which everyone had enjoyed enormously.

There had been rather a long pause when it came to Paddington's turn and the Browns were beginning to get impatient. Paddington had explained that it was a very secret dish and so they'd had to turn their backs on the camp-fire and promise not to look while he cooked it.

There seemed to be a lot of stirring and clanking going on behind them, not to mention some very heavy breathing, but the smell which wafted on the breeze was certainly making their mouths water and they were all looking forward to discovering what was his secret dish.

Mrs. Brown cheated and stole an anxious glance over her shoulder to where Paddington was bending over his saucepan. He had a large recipe book in one paw and he appeared to be poking something cautiously with a stick while he sniffed it.

" I hope he doesn't set light to his whiskers," she said. " He's awfully near the flames."

" It doesn't smell like burning whiskers," said Mr. Brown. " In fact I must say it smells rather good. I wonder what it is? "

" Perhaps it's something he found in his suitcase," replied Mrs. Bird.

Mr. Brown looked slightly less enthusiastic at Mrs. Bird's remark. " Something he found in his suitcase? " he repeated.

" Well, I can't think what else it can be," said Mrs. Bird. " *I* haven't given him anything to cook and we haven't stopped near a shop."

" I bet it's got marmalade in it," said Jonathan. " Paddington's things always have marmalade."

Fortunately for everyone's peace of mind, before they had time to think too much about it Paddington stood up and announced that everything was ready and they could all turn round.

Mrs. Brown looked suspiciously at Paddington as they gathered round the saucepan. There were one or two gravy splashes sticking to his whiskers and something which looked remarkably like flour, but otherwise everything seemed quite normal.

Paddington looked most important as the Browns

queued up with their plates. "It's a special French recipe," he explained as he served them all with generous helpings. "I found it in Mr. Gruber's cookery book."

He listened with pleasure to the gasps of delight from the others as they tasted his dish. Although he'd had several goes on Mrs. Bird's stove at one time and another it was the first time he had ever cooked anything over a camp-fire—especially anything quite so complicated as a French recipe—and although he had followed the instructions most carefully he was anxious in case he'd done something wrong. But first one and then another of the Browns congratulated him, and even Mrs. Bird was full of praise.

" I don't know what it is," she said, " but I couldn't have done better myself! " Which, from Mrs. Bird, was high praise indeed.

" Delicious," said Mr. Brown. " Very meaty and done to a turn."

" In fact," he continued, as he held out his plate for a second helping, " I don't know when I've tasted anything quite so nice before.

" Most unusual," he went on, as he wiped his plate clean with a piece of bread and looked hopefully at the saucepan once again. " What was it called, Paddington? "

" They're called *esca . . . esca . . .* something, Mr. Brown," said Paddington, consulting his cookery book. " *Escargots.*"

" *Escargots?* " repeated Mr. Brown, dabbing at his moustache. " Very nice too. We must get some of those when we're back in England, Mary . . ." His voice trailed away as he looked at his wife. Mrs. Brown's face seemed to have gone a rather odd shade of green.

" Is anything the matter? " he asked, looking most concerned. " You look quite ill."

" Henry! " exclaimed Mrs. Brown. " Don't you know what *escargots* are? "

" Er . . . no," said Mr. Brown. " Sounds familiar but I can't say that I do. Why? "

" They're snails," said Mrs. Brown.

" *What*! " exclaimed Mr. Brown. " Snails? Did you say *snails*? "

" Crikey! " groaned Jonathan. " Snails! "

" But where on earth did you get them, Paddington? " asked Mr. Brown, voicing all their thoughts.

" Oh, they didn't cost very much, Mr. Brown," said Paddington hurriedly, misunderstanding the look of alarm on everyone's face. " The man in the shop let me have them cheap because the shells were cracked. I think they were a very good bargain."

Much to Paddington's surprise his remark was greeted by renewed groans from the Browns, and he looked most upset at the sight of them all rolling on the grass holding their stomachs.

" To think I had a second helping," said Mr. Brown. " I'm sure I've been poisoned. There's a funny thumping noise in my head."

" Did you say the man in the shop? " asked Mrs. Bird suddenly.

" That's a point," said Mr. Brown as he sat up. " What shop? "

Paddington thought for a moment. He had been

63

hoping to save his news of the village until after the meal as a special surprise for the Browns and he was most disappointed at the thought of having to tell them straight away, but before he had time to answer, Mrs. Bird suddenly began waving her sunshade in the air and pointing in the direction of the hill.

" Gracious me! " she exclaimed. " What on earth's going on over there? "

" Good heavens! No wonder I had a thumping noise in my head," said Mr. Brown, as he followed the direction of Mrs. Bird's sunshade to where an enormous tractor was coming over the brow of the hill, followed by a long line of people. " It looks like a procession of some kind."

The Browns watched in fascination as the crowd drew nearer and nearer and finally came to a halt in front of them. The leader, a fat, jolly-looking man in white overalls and a tall chef's hat, bowed low in Paddington's direction.

" Ah, Monsieur le Bear," he exclaimed, beaming all over his face as he held out his hand. " We meet again! "

" Hallo, Mr. Dupont," cried Paddington, hurriedly wiping the gravy stains off his paw before offering it.

" Would someone mind pinching me? " said Mr. Brown, as he looked at the others. " I think I must be dreaming."

" Welcome to St. Castille," said Monsieur Dupont, as he advanced on Mr. Brown. " Please, we have come to see the stage-coach which has lost its wheel. Monsieur le Bear has already explained to us all about the matter and we are most anxious to help."

" The *stage-coach*? " repeated Mr. Brown, looking more and more mystified. " What stage-coach? "

Paddington took a deep breath. " I think perhaps I must have got my phrases mixed up by mistake, Mr. Brown," he said. " There wasn't a chapter on motor cars having a puncture so I used the one on stage-coaches instead."

It was all a bit difficult to explain, and Paddington wasn't quite sure where to start first.

" I think," said Mr. Brown, turning to Monsieur Dupont, the baker, " we had better sit down. I have a feeling this may take rather a long time."

" You know," said Mr. Brown much later that evening as they sat outside the hotel in Paddington's village taking a nightcap before going to bed, " I'll say this for Paddington, things may get complicated now and then but they have a habit of turning out right in the end."

" Bears always fall on their feet," said Mrs. Bird darkly. " I've said it before and I'll say it again."

" I vote we stay here," said Mr. Brown. " It wasn't on the itinerary, but I don't think we could find anything nicer."

" Hear, hear! " said Mrs. Bird.

After all the excitement of the afternoon everything

seemed particularly quiet and peaceful. The stars were shining in a cloudless sky, the sound of gay music from a nearby café filled the air, and at the end of the street leading down to the harbour they could see the lights from the fishing boats as they bobbed up and down in the water.

In fact, apart from the music, the only sound to disturb the night air was the steady scratching of the old nib on Paddington's pen and the occasional sigh as he dipped a paw into his marmalade jar.

When the Browns had discovered where Paddington bought his snails they had suddenly felt much better. It was a most respectable-looking shop and Monsieur Dupont assured them it was noted for its snails, so by popular vote Paddington had been given the prize for the best dish of the day.

After a great deal of thought and peering in shop windows he had used the money in order to buy some stamps and two picture postcards, one for his Aunt Lucy in Peru and one for Mr. Gruber.

They were big postcards—two of the biggest he had ever seen. Apart from having a space on which to write, they each had eleven different pictures on the front which showed scenes of the village and the surrounding countryside. One of the pictures showed Monsieur Dupont's bakery and by looking at it very hard Paddington could see some buns in the window which he thought Mr. Gruber would find very interesting.

There was even a picture of the hotel, and he carefully drew a large cross against one of the windows and wrote the words MY ROOM at the side.

Looking at the cards, Paddington decided they were very good value indeed and he felt sure his Aunt Lucy would be most surprised to get one all the way from France.

All the same, there had been so many happenings that day, and some of them were so difficult to explain, he felt it was going to be a job getting them all in— even on a bargain size postcard.

CHAPTER FIVE

'Paddington and the "Pardon"

THE BROWNS soon settled down in the village and in no time at all it seemed as if they had always lived there. The news that a young English bear gentleman was staying at the hotel quickly spread, and Paddington was soon a popular figure in the streets, especially in the early mornings when he did his shopping before going down to the beach.

He paid a visit to his new friend, Monsieur Dupont, most days. Monsieur Dupont spoke very good English

68

and they had several chats together on the subject of buns. Monsieur Dupont not only showed Paddington round his ovens but he also promised to bake some special English buns for his elevenses into the bargain.

" After all," he explained, " it is not every day we have a bear staying in St. Castille." And he put a notice in his shop window saying that in future special buns made to the recipe of a young English bear of quality would be on sale.

There were so many new and interesting things to see and do that Paddington had to sit up late in bed several nights running in order to write everything in his scrapbook while it was still fresh in his mind.

One morning he was wakened early by the sound of shouting and banging outside the hotel, and when he looked out of the window he discovered to his astonishment that a great change had come over the village.

It was always busy, with people hurrying to and fro about their daily tasks, but on this particular morning it seemed to be twice as busy as usual. Even the people were dressed in quite a different way. Instead of their blue overalls and red jerseys the fishermen all had on their best suits, and the women and girls were wearing dresses covered in stiff white lace with tall lace hats to match.

Nearly all the fruit and vegetable stalls had gone

and their place had been taken by other stalls decor-
ated with coloured flags and striped awnings, and
laden with boxes of sweets and row upon row of wax
candles.

It was all most unusual, and after a quick wash
Paddington hurried downstairs to investigate the
matter.

Madame Penet, the owner of the hotel, was at her
desk in the entrance hall when Paddington entered
and she looked at him rather doubtfully when he con-

sulted his phrase-book. Madame Penet's English was no better than Paddington's French and things always seemed to go wrong when they tried to talk to each other.

"It is," she began, in reply to his question, "'ow do you say? . . . a *pardon*."

"That's all right," said Paddington politely. "I only wondered what was happening. It looks very interesting."

Madame Penet nodded. "That is right," she said. "It is, 'ow do you say? . . . a *pardon*."

Paddington gave Madame Penet a hard stare as he backed away. Although he was a polite bear he was beginning to get a bit fed up with raising his hat and saying "pardon" in return, and so he hurried outside and across the square in order to consult Monsieur Dupont on the subject.

To his surprise when he entered the shop he made an even more startling discovery, for in place of the white smock and hat which he usually wore, Monsieur Dupont had on a very smart dark blue uniform covered in gold braid.

Monsieur Dupont laughed when he saw the expression on Paddington's face. "It is all to do with the *pardon*, Monsieur le Bear," he said.

And he went on to explain that in France *pardon* was the name given to a very special festival, and that in Brittany in particular there were *pardons* for many different reasons. There were *pardons* for fishermen and farmers, and there was even a *pardon* for the birds, not to mention horses and cattle.

" In the morning," said Monsieur Dupont, " there is always a procession, when everyone goes to church, and afterwards there is much celebration.

" This year," he went on, " we have a Fair and a firework display. Why, there is even a parade of the village band! "

Monsieur Dupont drew himself up to his full height. " That is why I am in uniform, Monsieur le Bear," he exclaimed proudly. " For I am the leader of the band! "

Paddington looked most impressed as he listened to Monsieur Dupont, and after thanking him for all his trouble he hurried back to the hotel in order to tell the others.

Most days the Browns went down to the beach, but when they heard Paddington's news they quickly changed their plans. After a hurried breakfast they joined the rest of the villagers in going to church, and that afternoon, by popular vote, they made their way towards a field just outside the village where the Fair was taking place.

Paddington stood in a trance as he gazed at the sight which met his eyes. It was the first time he had been to a Fair and he didn't remember ever having seen or heard anything quite like it before.

There were huge wheels soaring up into the sky. There were gaily-painted swings and slides. There were roundabouts carrying dozens of shrieking, laughing people round and round as they clung to wooden horses painted all the colours of the rainbow. There were coconut-shies and side-shows. Everywhere there were coloured lights flashing on and off, and in the centre of it all there was a huge organ playing gay music as it let out clouds of steam. In fact there were so many things crammed into such a small space it was difficult to decide what to do first.

In the end, after testing the slides and swings a number of times, Paddington turned his attention to one of the roundabouts, and when he discovered that bears under sixteen were allowed on for half-price on *pardon* days he had several more goes for good measure.

It was when he came off the roundabout for the last time and stood watching Mr. Brown, Jonathan and Judy while they had a go, that he suddenly spied for the first time a most interesting-looking small striped tent which stood slightly apart from the rest of the Fair. There were several notices pinned to the outside, most of them printed in foreign languages, but there was one written in English which caught his eye at once and he read it carefully. It said:

MADAME ZAZA
International Fortune Teller
PALMS READ
CRYSTAL-GAZING
SATISFACTION GUARANTEED

Pasted across the bottom was a smaller notice which had the words ENGLISH SPOKEN printed in red.

Mrs. Brown followed Paddington's gaze as he lifted up the tent flap and peered inside. " It says she reads palms," she remarked doubtfully, " but I should be careful—paws might be more expensive."

Mrs. Brown wasn't at all sure it would be a good thing for Paddington to have his fortune told—he got into enough trouble as it was without looking into the future. But before she had time to make him change his mind the tent flap had closed behind him. Paddington had never before heard of anyone having their paw read and he was anxious to investigate the matter.

After the strong sunlight it was dark inside the tent, and as he groped his way forward he had to blink several times before he could make out a shadowy figure sitting behind a small, velvet-covered table.

Madame Zaza had her eyes closed and she was breathing heavily. After waiting impatiently for a few moments Paddington gave her a poke with his paw and then raised his hat.

" Please," he announced, " I've come to have my paw read."

Madame Zaza jumped. " *Comment!* " she exclaimed hoarsely.

" Come on? " said Paddington, looking puzzled. There was hardly space inside the tent for the two of them, let alone room to go anywhere, so he tried climbing on the table as he explained once again what he had come for.

"Mind my crystal ball," cried Madama Zaza, breaking into English as the table rocked. "They're very expensive.

"I didn't realise you were a foreigner," she continued. "Otherwise I would have spoken to you in your own language."

"A foreigner!" exclaimed Paddington hotly. "I'm not a foreigner. I've come from England!"

"You're a foreigner when you're in another country," said Madame Zaza sternly. "And '*comment*' doesn't mean you're supposed to climb all over my table!"

Paddington sighed as he climbed down off the table. He didn't think much of French as a language. Everything seemed to have the opposite meaning to the one he was used to.

"Anyway, I don't usually do bears," said Madame Zaza cautiously. "But as you're on holiday, if you like to cross my palm with silver I'll see what I can do to oblige."

Paddington undid his suitcase and taking out a sixpence passed it over Madame Zaza's outstretched hand before quickly putting it away again. Having his paw read was much cheaper than he had expected.

Madame Zaza gave Paddington a startled look.

" You're supposed to stop half-way and drop it in," she exclaimed.

Paddington gave Madame Zaza one of his special hard stares in return before he undid his suitcase once again and handed back the sixpence.

" I don't usually take foreign coins either," said Madame Zaza, biting the sixpence to make sure it was good, " but it seems to be all right. Let me see your paw. I'll read the lines on that first."

As Paddington held out his paw, Madame Zaza took it in her hand. After staring at it disbelievingly for a moment she rubbed her eyes and then took a magnifying glass out of her pocket.

" You seem to have a very long life-line," she said, " even for a bear. I've never seen such a thick one before, and it runs the whole length of your paw."

Paddington followed her gaze with interest. " I don't think it *is* a life-line," he said. " I think it's an old marmalade chunk."

" *An old marmalade chunk?* " repeated Madame Zaza in a dazed voice.

" That's right," said Paddington. " It got stuck on at breakfast and I must have forgotten to wash it off."

Madame Zaza passed a trembling hand across her brow. It seemed to be getting very hot inside the tent. " Well," she said, " I certainly can't read your paw if it's covered in old marmalade peel. I'm afraid you'll have to pay extra and have the crystal ball."

Paddington looked at her suspiciously as he withdrew another sixpence from his case. He was beginning to wish he hadn't thought of having his fortune told.

Madame Zaza snatched the money from him and then drew the crystal ball towards her. " First you must tell me when your birthday is," she said.

" June and December," replied Paddington.

" June *and* December? " repeated Madame Zaza. " But you can't have *two* birthdays. Nobody has more than one."

" Bears do," said Paddington firmly. " Bears always have two birthdays."

" Then that makes it more difficult," said Madame Zaza. " And I certainly can't guarantee results."

She waved her hands through the air several times and then stared hard at the ball. " It says you are going on a journey," she began, in a strange, distant voice, " quite soon! " She looked up at Paddington and added hopefully, " I think you ought to start right away."

" I'm going on a journey? " exclaimed Paddington, looking most surprised. " But I've only just been on one. I've come all the way from Windsor Gardens! Does it say where I'm going? "

Madame Zaza consulted her glass once more, and as she did so a crafty look came over her face. " No," she said, " but wherever it is things will certainly go off with a bang! "

Madame Zaza had remembered the firework display that was due to take place that evening, and it seemed a very good answer to Paddington's question. But as she gazed at her crystal ball a puzzled look gradually came over her face. After breathing on the glass she gave it a polish with the end of her shawl. " I don't remember this ever happening before," she exclaimed excitedly. " I can see another bear! "

" I don't think it's another one," said Paddington, as he stood on his suitcase and peered over Madame Zaza's shoulder. " I think it's me. But I can't see anything else."

Madame Zaza hastily covered the crystal ball with her shawl. " It's fading," she said crossly. " I think my palm needs crossing again."

" *Again?* " said Paddington suspiciously. " But it's only just been crossed! "

" Again," said Madame Zaza firmly. " Sixpence doesn't last very long."

Paddington looked very disappointed as he backed away from Madame Zaza, and he hurriedly dropped the tent flap before she could ask for any more money.

The Browns were standing by the roundabout chatting with Monsieur Dupont when Paddington came out of the tent and they looked up inquiringly as he hurried across to join them.

" Well, dear? " asked Mrs. Brown. " How did you get on? "

" Not very well, Mrs. Brown," said Paddington sadly. " It wasn't very good value. I think my lines must have been crossed."

Monsieur Dupont raised his hands in sympathy. " Ah, Monsieur le Bear," he exclaimed. " If only our troubles could be solved by looking into a crystal ball life would be very simple. I, too, would like to see into the future! "

Monsieur Dupont had a very worried look on his face and he had just been explaining to the Browns all about a problem which had to do with the celebrations that evening.

" Once a year," he said, as he repeated the story for Paddington's benefit, " we have a parade of the village band and to-night, of all nights, the man who plays the big drum has been taken ill! "

" What a shame," said Mrs. Brown. " It must be very disappointing."

" Can't you find *anyone* else? " asked Mr. Brown.

Monsieur Dupont shook his head sadly. " They are all much too busy enjoying themselves at the Fair," he said. " And already we are late for rehearsals."

As he listened to the others talking Paddington's eyes got larger and larger, and several times he looked over his shoulder at Madame Zaza's tent as if he could hardly believe his ears.

"Perhaps I could help, Mr. Dupont," he said excitedly when the baker had finished talking.

"*You*, Monsieur le Bear?" said Monsieur Dupont, looking most surprised. "But what could you do?"

Everyone listened with growing astonishment as Paddington explained about his "fortune" and how Madame Zaza had said he would be going on a journey and that everything would go off with a bang.

When he had finished, Monsieur Dupont stroked his chin thoughtfully. "It is certainly most strange," he said. "It is *extraordinaire!*"

Monsieur Dupont grew more and more enthusiastic as he considered the matter. "I have never before heard of a bear playing in a band," he said. "It would be a great attraction."

The Browns exchanged glances. "I'm sure it's a very great honour," said Mrs. Brown doubtfully. "But is it wise?"

"What is a band," cried Monsieur Dupont, waving his arms dramatically in the air, "without someone at the back who can go *boum, boum, boum?*"

The Browns were silent. There didn't seem to be any answer to Monsieur Dupont's question.

"Oh, well," said Mr. Brown. "It's your band!"

"In that case," said Monsieur Dupont briskly, "the matter is settled!"

The Browns watched anxiously as Monsieur Dupont and Paddington hurried off to start their rehearsals.

The idea of Paddington becoming a member of the village band gave rise to thoughts of all sorts of awful possibilities.

But as the afternoon wore on, despite their first misgivings, they became quite excited at the idea and by the time night fell and they settled themselves on the hotel balcony in readiness for the grand march past even Mr. Brown kept repeating how much he was looking forward to it all.

In the distance they could hear the musicians tuning up their instruments, and several times there was a loud bang as Paddington tested his drum for the last time.

" I only hope he doesn't make a mistake and ruin everything," said Mrs. Brown. " He's not really very musical."

" If some of the banging that goes on at home is anything to go by," said Mrs. Bird, looking up from her knitting, " there's nothing to worry about! "

Suddenly, after a short pause, there was a great flurry of sound and a cheer went up from the waiting villagers as the band, led by Monsieur Dupont, entered the square to the tune of a rousing march.

Monsieur Dupont himself looked very impressive as he threw his stick in the air with a flourish and caught it with one hand as it came down, but the biggest cheer of all was reserved for Paddington as he came into view behind a very large drum. The news

that the young English bear gentleman had stepped
in at the last moment to save the day had quickly
gone the rounds and a large crowd had turned out to
witness the event.

Paddington felt most important when he heard the
applause, and he waved his paws several times in
acknowledgement in between hitting the drum,
reserving a special wave for the Browns as he passed
the hotel.

" Well," said Mrs. Bird proudly, as the band disappeared from view up the street, " that bear may only be bringing up the rear, but I thought he was better than all the rest put together! "

" I've managed to get some pictures," said Mr. Brown, lowering his camera, " but I'm afraid they're only back views."

" You'll be able to get some front ones in a minute, Dad," said Jonathan. " I think they're on their way back."

Mr. Brown hurriedly reloaded his camera as the sound of the music got louder again. Having finished off the first tune with a series of loud crashes, the band had broken into another march and was heading back towards the square.

" Paddington doesn't seem quite so loud now," said Mrs. Brown as they settled back in their seats. " I hope he isn't having trouble with his sticks."

" Perhaps his paws are getting tired," said Judy.

" Crikey! " exclaimed Jonathan, jumping up as the band came into view again. " He isn't with them any more."

" What's that? " exclaimed Mr. Brown, lowering his camera. " Not there! But he must be."

The Browns peered anxiously over the edge of the

balcony, and even Monsieur Dupont glanced over his shoulder several times before he brought the band to a halt in the middle of the square, but Paddington was nowhere to be seen.

"That's funny," said Mr. Brown, cupping a hand to his ear as the music stopped. "I can still hear something."

The others listened intently. The sound Mr. Brown had heard seemed to be coming from the far side of the village. It was getting fainter and fainter all the time, but it was definitely that of a drum.

"Crumbs! I bet that's Paddington," said Judy. "He must have carried straight on by mistake when the others turned back."

"We'd better go after him then," said Mr. Brown urgently. "There's no knowing where he might end up."

The Browns began to look worried as the full meaning of the situation sank in. Even Paddington himself, had he been in a position to see what was going on, would have agreed that things looked rather black, but as it was he plodded on his way blissfully unaware of the turn of events.

All in all, what with the Fair and the band rehearsal

he had spent a most enjoyable day, but now that the first excitement of the march past was over he was beginning to wish it would soon come to an end.

To start with, the drum was much too large and heavy for his liking, and having short legs made it difficult to keep in step. The drum was strapped to his front and during rehearsals he had been able to rest it on his suitcase, but now he was on the march it was much higher and he couldn't even begin to see over the top. Apart from having no idea where he was, it was getting very hot inside his duffle coat and the jogging had made the hood fall over his ears so that he couldn't hear the other musicians.

Monsieur Dupont had taken great pains to explain how important an instrument the drum was and that even when the band stopped playing it still had to be banged so that the others could keep in step, but as far as Paddington could make out for the past five minutes it had been all drum and no band and he was beginning to get a bit fed up.

The farther along the road he went the heavier it became and, to add to his troubles, as his knees began to sag under the weight, the duffle coat hood fell completely over his head and stayed there.

Just as he was trying to make up his mind whether or not to call out for help, matters were suddenly decided for him. One moment he was plodding along the road, the next moment his foot met nothing but air. In fact, he hardly had time to let out a gasp of surprise before everything seemed to turn upside down, and before he knew where he was he found himself lying on his back with what seemed like a ton weight on top of him.

Paddington lay where he was for some moments gasping for breath before he cautiously pulled back his duffle coat hood and peered out. To his surprise, neither Monsieur Dupont nor the rest of the band were anywhere in sight. In fact, the only things he could see at all were the moon and the stars in the sky above him. Worse still, when he tried to get up again he found he couldn't, for the drum was resting on his stomach and try as he might he couldn't move it.

Paddington let out a deep sigh as he lay back in the road. " Oh, dear! " he said, addressing the world in general. " I'm in trouble again! "

" What a good thing you kept on banging the drum," said Mrs. Brown thankfully. " You might have stayed there all night."

It was some while later and everyone had gathered in the hotel lounge in order to hear Paddington's explanations of the evening's events and how he had come to be rescued. Monsieur Dupont in particular was very relieved to see Paddington again for he felt responsible for the whole affair.

" I think I must have put my paw in a pot-hole by

mistake, Mrs. Brown," said Paddington. "Then I couldn't get up again because the drum was on top of me."

Mrs. Brown wanted to ask Paddington why he hadn't tried undoing the straps, but she tactfully kept silent. As it was, far too many people were talking at once and quite a crowd had collected in order to congratulate Paddington and Monsieur Dupont on their march past.

In any case Paddington was much too busy with his own problems and from a distance he looked as if he was trying to turn himself inside out.

"It's all right, Mrs. Brown," he said hurriedly, when he saw her look of concern. "I was only testing the lines on my paw."

"Well, I hope you found something interesting after all that," said Mrs. Bird. "It looked most uncomfortable."

"I'm not sure," said Paddington hopefully, "but it looked like a firework!"

"H'mm!" said Mrs. Bird darkly as a sudden "woosh" came from outside and the first rocket of the evening lit up the sky. "It sounds suspiciously like a bear's wishful thinking to me!"

But her words fell on deaf ears for Paddington had already disappeared outside, closely followed by Jonathan and Judy, with Mr. Brown and Monsieur Dupont bringing up the rear.

Paddington liked fireworks and now that he had

recovered from his adventure with the dr.   was looking forward to the evening display. Judging by the noise going on in the square outside the hotel, he had a feeling French fireworks might be very good value indeed and he didn't want to miss a single moment of the fun.

A Spot of Fishing

" How ABOUT a spot of fishing to-day? " asked Mr.
Brown at breakfast one morning.

Mr. Brown's query was greeted in various ways by
the other members of the family. Mrs. Brown and
Mrs. Bird exchanged anxious glances, Jonathan and
Judy let out whoops of delight, while Paddington
nearly fell off his seat with excitement.

" What are we going to fish for? " asked Mrs.
Brown, hoping her husband might suggest something
safe near the seashore.

"Mackerel," said Mr. Brown vaguely. "Or we might even try for some sardines. Anyway, all those in favour raise their right hand."

Mr. Brown looked pleased at the response to his idea. "That's four to two in favour," he said.

"It's two all," said Mrs. Bird sternly. "Bears who raise both their paws at the same time are disqualified."

"Well, I haven't voted yet," said Mr. Brown, putting up his own hand, "so that's still three to two.

"There's a nice little island just outside the bay," he continued. "We can sail out there and make it our base."

"Did you say *sail* out there, Henry?" asked Mrs. Brown nervously.

"That's right," said Mr. Brown. "I met Admiral Grundy just before breakfast and he's invited us out for the day."

Mrs. Brown and Mrs. Bird began to look even less enthusiastic at Mr. Brown's last remark, and even Paddington's whiskers drooped noticeably into his roll and marmalade.

Admiral Grundy was a retired English naval officer who lived in a house called the Crow's Nest on the cliffs just outside the village. The Browns had met him on one or two occasions and he had a voice like a rusty fog-horn which always made them rather nervous.

The first time he had bellowed at them so loudly

from the top of the cliff that Mrs. Brown had been quite worried in case there was a fall of rock, and Paddington had dropped an ice-cream cone into the sea in his fright.

" Been watchin' you for the last three days through me telescope," he'd roared at Mr. Brown. " Knew by your shorts you must be English. Thought I saw a bear gallivantin' about on the beach. Couldn't believe me eyes! "

" I think his bark's worse than his bite," said Mr. Brown. " And he seems very keen on our going out with him. I don't suppose he sees many English people now he's retired."

" H'mm! " said Mrs. Bird mysteriously, " I can see we've got some preparations to make." And with that she left the table and disappeared upstairs only to return a few minutes later armed with a small parcel which she handed to Paddington.

" Something told me we might be going sailing," she said. " Sea-water makes bears' fur sticky, so I made a sea-going outfit before we left out of one of Jonathan's old cycling capes."

Paddington gasped with astonishment when he untied the parcel and saw what was inside, and everyone stood round admiring while he donned a pair of oilskin leggings, a jacket and a sou'wester.

" Thank you very much, Mrs. Bird," he said gratefully, as he made some final adjustments to his braces.

" That settles it," said Mr. Brown. " We shall simply *have* to go sailing now! "

After they had collected their belongings the Browns made their way down the winding cobbled street leading to the harbour and Paddington followed them in a daze. To have one surprise was a nice way to start any day, but to be told he was going sailing *and* to have a new outfit at the same time was doubly exciting.

Paddington was very keen on boats and harbours, and he liked the one at St. Castille in particular for it was quite different to anything he had ever seen before in his travels. For one thing the fishermen used most unusual light blue nets which looked very gay when they were hung out to dry. And even the men themselves were different, for instead of wearing dark blue jerseys and rubber boots like most fishermen, they had red jackets and wooden clogs called " sabots."

Paddington had spent a lot of his time sitting on the quayside with the Browns watching the activities in the harbour as the sardine boats came and went, and he was looking forward to the day's outing.

Admiral Grundy was already on board his yacht when the Browns arrived, and as they rounded the corner he gave a start and then fixed Paddington with a steely look from beneath his bushy eyebrows.

" Shiver me timbers! " he exploded. " What's this? Expectin' a gale? "

" Shiver your timbers, Mr. Grundy? " exclaimed Paddington with interest.   He peered hard at the Admiral's boat but it appeared to be all in one piece and the planks seemed well stuck together.

" I think he's surprised at your oilskins," whispered Judy, as the Admiral looked up at the sun and then back at Paddington.

" My oilskins? " said Paddington hotly, giving the Admiral a hard stare back.   " They're some of Mrs. Bird's specials! "

Recovering himself, the Admiral held out his hand gallantly to Mrs. Bird.   " Welcome aboard, ma'am," he exclaimed.   " Hope I haven't offended you.   Come along now.   Women and bears first."

" You can go up for'ard, bear," he said as Paddington clambered aboard.   " Keep a sharp look-out— and listen for me instructions."

After touching the brim of his sou'wester with his paw, Paddington hurried along the deck until he reached the front of the boat.   He wasn't quite sure what he was supposed to look out for but he felt very pleased he'd brought his opera-glasses along and he spent several moments peering through them at the horizon.

Although he didn't want to offend Mrs. Bird after all the trouble she had taken, he was beginning to wish he'd taken Admiral Grundy's advice and kept his sailing outfit until a storm blew up.   Apart from the fact that it was a hot day, his braces kept slipping off his shoulders and he had to hold his trousers up with one paw, which made keeping a lookout very difficult.

He was suddenly startled out of his daydreams by a roar from the back of the yacht.

" Stand by for'ard! " bellowed the Admiral as he inspected his ship.

" Watch the burgee," he shouted, pointing to a small triangular flag which flew at the mast-head. " Tells you which way the wind's blowin'," he explained to Mrs. Bird, who was sheltering in the stern beneath her sunshade. " Most important! "

" Get ready to splice the mainbrace down below," he called to Mr. Brown, who was somewhere in the cabin. " Stand by to cast off up for'ard, bear! "

From his position in the front of the Admiral's yacht, Paddington was getting more and more confused by all the shouting. Setting sail was much more complicated than he had imagined.

First of all he thought the Admiral had said something about watching a birdy, but the only birds he could see were sea-gulls and most of those seemed to be asleep.

Then the Admiral had bellowed something about splicing his braces.

Paddington was most surprised by the last order for although his trousers were getting lower and lower, he hadn't realised anyone else had noticed and he hastily picked up a coil of rope and began tying it round his middle to be on the safe side.

"Stand by!" bellowed the Admiral. "I'm goin' to haul up me mainsail."

"Nothin' like a good sailin' craft," he continued with satisfaction as he pulled away at the rope. "Can't stand engines meself."

"I must say it's a lovely sight," began Mrs. Brown as the large white sail billowed out in the breeze. She broke off and stared at the Admiral. "Is anything the matter?" she asked.

"Where's that young bear feller of yours got to?" exploded the Admiral. "Don't tell me he's fallen overboard!"

"Good gracious!" exclaimed Mrs. Bird anxiously. "Where on earth can he have got to?"

The Browns looked over the side into the water but there was neither sight nor sound of Paddington.

"Can't see any bubbles," said the Admiral. "And as for hearin' anything—couldn't hear a ship's siren with all that jabberin' goin' on ashore—let alone a bear's cries!"

The Browns looked up. Now that the Admiral mentioned it, there did seem to be a lot of noise going on. Quite a number of the fishermen on the quay were waving their arms and several were pointing up at the sky.

"Good grief!" exploded the Admiral as he stood up and shaded his eyes against the sun. "He's up aloft. Got himself hoisted to me mainmast!"

"I was only splicing my braces," gasped Paddington,

looking most offended as he was lowered back down on to the deck. " I was having trouble with my oil-skins and I think I must have picked up the wrong rope by mistake."

" I think," said Mrs. Bird, quickly pouring oil on troubled waters before the Admiral had time to speak, " you'd better sit in the back with me out of harm's way."

Already quite a large crowd had collected on the quayside and she didn't like the look on the Admiral's face. It seemed to have gone a rather nasty shade of purple.

Paddington dusted himself down and then settled thankfully in the seat alongside Mrs. Bird while order was restored and the Admiral once more made ready to sail.

Within a matter of moments everything was ship-shape and before long they found themselves skimming through the open water outside the harbour.

While Jonathan and Judy sat on the deck watching the wash of the wave breaking over the bow of the yacht, Mr. Brown set up his rod and line, and even Paddington had a go over the stern with a piece of string and a bent pin which Mrs. Bird found in her handbag.

It was all so new and interesting that it seemed no time at all before they found themselves on the island.

Apart from all the Admiral's things, Mr. Brown

had brought along a tent and a large hamper of food
which Mrs. Bird had bought in the village store, and
while Jonathan, Judy and Paddington made ready
to explore the island, the Admiral and Mr. Brown
began unloading the yacht.

It was as they turned to go back for their second
trip that the Admiral suddenly let out an extra loud
bellow and began pointing out to sea as he danced
up and down the beach.

" It's adrift! " he cried. " Me yacht's adrift! "

The Browns followed the direction of the Admiral's
gaze with alarm only to see the yacht dancing on the
waves some distance away as it headed out to sea.

" Shiver me timbers! " roared the Admiral. " Didn't
anyone tie it up? "

The Browns looked at each other. In the excitement of landing on the island they had left it to the
Admiral.

" We thought you'd done it," said Mr. Brown.

" Fifty years at sea," growled the Admiral, stomp-
ing up and down the beach. " Never lost a ship yet,
let alone been marooned. What a crew! "

" Can't you send up a distress signal or something? "
asked Mrs. Brown unhappily.

" Can't," growled the Admiral. " Me flares are on
board! "

" So are my matches," said Mr. Brown. " So we
can't even light a bonfire."

Admiral Grundy stomped up and down the beach

several more times growling to himself before he stopped and pointed to Mr. Brown's tent. " I'll set up me headquarters on the grass at the top of the beach," he exclaimed. " Must have a bit of peace and quiet while I think up some way of letting the johnnies on the mainland know what's happened."

" I'll help if you like, Mr. Grundy," said Paddington, anxious to lend a paw.

" Thank you, bear," said the Admiral gruffly. " But you'll have to be careful with your knots. Don't want it blowin' over as soon as I get inside."

Leaving the Browns in a forlorn group on the beach as they discussed the prospect of spending a night on the island, the Admiral picked up the tent and headed towards the top of the beach closely followed by Paddington.

Paddington was very interested in the subject of Mr. Brown's tent. He had come across it once or twice when he'd been exploring the attic at Windsor Gardens, but he'd never seen it in use before. When they reached the grass he sat down on a nearby rock and watched carefully while the Admiral undid the carrying case and spread a large sheet of white canvas over the ground, together with several lengths of wooden pole and a number of ropes.

After joining the wooden poles together into two lengths, the Admiral fitted the canvas sheet over them and then lifted the whole lot into the air.

" I'll hold the poles, bear," he roared as he disap-

peared inside, " if you'll fix the guy-ropes. You'll
find some stakes in the bag."

Paddington jumped up from the rock. He wasn't
at all sure what guy-ropes were, let alone stakes, but
he was glad to be able to do something useful at last,
and as he hurried forward and peered in the bag he
was even more pleased to see that as well as a mallet
and some pieces of wood there was a book of
instructions.

Paddington liked instruction books—especially
when there were plenty of pictures—and Mr. Brown's
seemed to have a great many. On the cover there was
one which showed a man hammering the pieces of
wood into the ground, and although the man in the
picture wore shorts and was fat and jolly—not a bit
like the Admiral, who was very gruff—he felt sure it
would be a great help.

" What's goin' on, bear? " called the Admiral in a
muffled voice. " Shake a leg there. I can't hold on
much longer."

Paddington looked up and saw to his surprise that
the Admiral and his tent were no longer where they
had started off. There was a strong breeze blowing
now that they were away from the beach and the
Admiral seemed to be having some difficulty in
staying upright as the canvas billowed out like a sail.

" Hold on, Mr. Grundy," cried Paddington,
waving his mallet in the air. " I'm coming."

After consulting the instructions several more times

he picked up a pawful of stakes and hurried across to where the Admiral was struggling.

Paddington was keen on hammering and he spent an enjoyable few minutes banging all the stakes into the ground and making fast the various ropes before pulling them tight as the Admiral had told him.

There were a great many ropes, in fact there seemed to be far more than there were in the picture, and Paddington had to make several trips back to the bag for more stakes so that it all took much longer than he had expected.

Apart from that the Admiral kept shouting for him to make haste so that he became more and more confused, and the knots—far from being neat and tidy like the ones in the instructions—began to look more and more like a piece of very old knitting that had gone wrong.

" Is that a new tent? " asked Mrs. Bird, as she viewed the goings on from the beach.

" No," replied Mr. Brown. " It's the same old one. Why do you ask? "

" It looks different to me," said Mrs. Bird. " It's a very odd shape. Sort of tall and baggy."

" Good heavens! " exclaimed Mr. Brown. " You're right."

" I think," said Mrs. Bird, " we'd better go and see what's happening. I don't like the look of things at all."

In saying she didn't like the look of things, Mrs.

Bird was echoing Paddington's thoughts as well as her own, for having at long last finished banging in all the stakes and tying all the knots he stood up to admire his handiwork only to find to his surprise that the Admiral was nowhere in sight.

Even the tent looked quite different to the one shown on the last page of the instructions. The one there was not unlike a small house, with the man in shorts looking as fresh as a daisy and smiling all over his face as he stepped out through a door in the

side and waved to a crowd of admiring onlookers. As
he mopped his brow and looked at Mr. Brown's tent,
even Paddington had to admit to himself that it was
more like a bundle of old washing with several lumps
sticking out the side.

He hurried all the way round peering at it closely,
but there was nowhere anyone could possibly crawl

through let alone any sign of a door. Worse still, far from there being any sign of a smiling Admiral, he seemed to have disappeared altogether.

Paddington anxiously tapped one of the lumps in the side with his hammer. "Are you there, Mr. Grundy?" he called.

"Grr," came an explosion from within. "THATWAS MYHEAD!"

Paddington jumped back as if he had been shot and nearly fell over one of the guy-ropes in his haste to escape.

"*Let me out, Bear!*" roared the Admiral. "*I'll have you in irons for this!*"

Paddington didn't like the sound of being put in irons at all and he hurriedly consulted the instruction book again in case he had turned over two pages at once by mistake, but there wasn't even a section on how to take the tent down again once it was up, let alone anything about missing campers.

He tried pulling hard on the guy-ropes, but it only seemed to make matters worse, and the harder he pulled the more the Admiral bellowed.

"Paddington!" exclaimed Mrs. Brown, as they reached him just in time to be greeted by a particularly loud yell from the Admiral. "What on earth's going on?"

"I don't know, Mrs. Brown," said Paddington. "I think I must have got my guys crossed. It's a bit difficult with paws."

" Crikey! " said Jonathan admiringly, as he bent down to examine the tent. " I'll say you have. I've never seen knots like these before. Not even in the Scouts."

" Good gracious! " said Mrs. Bird. " We'd better do something quickly. He'll suffocate."

One by one the Browns bent down and looked at the ropes, but the more they pulled and tugged the tighter became the knots and the fainter became the Admiral's gurgles.

It was just as they were giving up all hope of ever setting him free that a most unexpected interruption took place. The Browns had been so intent on the problem of untying Paddington's knots that they had quite failed to notice a lot of activity going on on the beach. The first they knew of it was when they heard voices close at hand and they looked up to find a group of fishermen from the village making their way towards them.

" We saw your signal for help, monsieur," said the leader in broken English.

" Our signal for help? " repeated Mr. Brown.

" That is right, monsieur," said the fisherman. " We saw it from many miles away. The young English bear from the hotel waving his white sheet in distress. And then we found Monsieur le Admiral's boat adrift so we came to the rescue."

Mr. Brown stood back while the fishermen gathered round the tent to inspect the knots. " I wonder whether it's just Paddington," he said. " Or whether all bears are born under a lucky star! "

" Grrmph!" growled the Admiral for the umpteenth time as the story of his rescue was repeated to him.

It had taken even the fishermen some while to undo Paddington's knots, and by the time he was set free the Admiral's face had been the colour of a freshly boiled lobster. But when he heard the news that his yacht had been found and was safely at anchor in the bay he soon grew calm again. As the day wore on he became quite jolly and even joined in a number of games on the beach.

" I suppose I ought to thank you, bear," he growled on the way back, as he held out his hand. " Could have done with a few more of your sort on board me ship in the old days. Enjoyed meself no end."

" That's all right, Mr. Grundy," said Paddington, offering his paw in return. He still wasn't quite sure why everyone was thanking him—especially as he had expected to be in trouble—but he wasn't the sort of bear to query his good fortune.

" Suppose you like cocoa? " growled the Admiral suddenly.

Paddington's eyes grew large. " Yes, please," he exclaimed. And even the Browns looked most surprised that the Admiral should know such a thing.

" Haven't travelled the seven seas without learnin' somethin' about bears' habits," said the Admiral.

He shaded his eyes as they entered the harbour mouth and the setting sun flickered for a moment behind the houses. " Don't suppose you've ever tasted real ship's cocoa," he said. " Make it meself in a bucket. How about comin' up to me cabin for a cup before you go to bed? "

To that the Browns gave an enthusiastic " Aye! Aye! " and even Paddington was allowed to raise both his paws in agreement. It had been a most exciting and enjoyable day, and although they had none of them so much as seen a glimpse of a sardine, let alone caught one, they all agreed there was nothing like a cup of real ship's cocoa to round things off in a proper seamanlike fashion.

CHAPTER SEVEN

Paddington Takes to the Road

MONSIEUR DUPONT looked at Paddington in amazement. "You mean to say, Monsieur le Bear," he exclaimed, "that you have never before heard of *le cyclisme*?"

"Never, Mr. Dupont," said Paddington earnestly.

"Poof!" cried Monsieur Dupont, raising his hands in the air. "Everyone should see a real bicycle race —it is most exciting. And you are indeed fortunate, for the one which is passing through our village to-morrow is the greatest of them all."

Monsieur Dupont paused to let his words sink in.
"It is called the 'Tour de France'," he continued
impressively. "It lasts for twenty days and people
come from all over the world to see it."

Paddington listened carefully as Monsieur Dupont
went on to explain what an honour it was to take part
in the race and how it would be going through the
village not once, but several times. "Up the hill,"
said Monsieur Dupont, "round the houses and down
the hill again. In that way everyone will have a chance
to see it.

"Why," he went on, "there is even a prize for
the champion rider down the hill into the village.
Think of that, Monsieur le Bear!"

At that moment Monsieur Dupont had to serve a
customer and so, after thanking him very much for
all his trouble, Paddington left the baker's shop and
hurried across the square to have another look at the
poster which had aroused his interest.

It was a large poster pasted on the side of a shop
and it showed a long, winding road crowded with
men on bicycles. All the men wore brightly-coloured
singlets and they had very earnest expressions on their
faces as they bent low over their handle-bars. They
seemed to have travelled a long way for they all looked
hot and tired, and one man was even eating a sandwich as he rode along.

Seeing the sandwich reminded Paddington that it

was nearly time for his elevenses, but before he went back into the hotel for his marmalade jar he spent some minutes with Mr. Gruber's phrase-book working out the words in small print at the bottom of the poster.

Paddington was most interested in the idea of anyone being able to win a prize simply by being the fastest person to ride down a hill on a bicycle. Not for the first time since he'd been on holiday he began to wish Mr. Gruber was on hand to explain matters to him.

There was a thoughtful expression on his face as he made his way to where the Browns were sitting outside the hotel, and several times during the next quarter of an hour he absent-mindedly dipped his paw into the cocoa by mistake instead of into his jar of marmalade.

Paddington was late arriving down at the beach that morning and the others had already been there some time when he came hurrying across the sand brandishing his bucket and spade and with a look on his face of a job well done.

" What on earth have you been doing, Paddington? " asked Mrs. Brown. " We were getting quite worried."

" Oh," said Paddington, waving his paws vaguely in the direction of the village. " Things in general, Mrs. Brown."

Mrs. Bird looked at him suspiciously. Now that

he was close to, she could see several dark patches on his fur which looked remarkably like old oil stains, but before she had time to examine them closely Paddington had made off again in the direction of the sea.

" You'd better not be late to-morrow, Paddington," called Mr. Brown. " It's the big cycle race. You mustn't miss that."

To everyone's astonishment, Mr. Brown's words had a very strange effect on Paddington, for he nearly fell over backwards with surprise and his face took on a most guilty expression as he collected himself and hurried into the water as fast as he could go, casting some anxious glances over his shoulder.

Mrs. Brown sighed. " There are times," she said, " when I would give anything to be able to read Paddington's mind. I'm sure it would be most interesting."

" H'mm! " said Mrs. Bird darkly. " There are times when I'm sure it's much better not to. We should never have a moment's peace. He looked much too pleased with himself just now for my liking."

With that the Browns settled down to enjoy themselves in the sun. With their holiday fast drawing to an end they wanted to make the most of it, and soon Paddington's odd behaviour was forgotten for the time being.

But Mrs. Brown was still worrying about the matter when they went to bed that evening. Paddington had disappeared upstairs unusually early and now there were some strange bumps coming from his room which she didn't like the sound of at all.

After spending some moments with her ear to the wall she beckoned her husband over. "I think he must be making some marmalade sandwiches, Henry," she said. "Listen."

"Making marmalade sandwiches?" repeated Mr. Brown. "I don't see how you can *hear* anyone make marmalade sandwiches."

"You can with Paddington," said Mrs. Brown. "You can hear the jars going. When he's eating it he just dips his paw in and you can hear the breathing, but when it's sandwiches he uses a spoon and you can hear the clinks as well."

"They must be big ones then," said Mr. Brown vaguely, as he stood up. "He's puffing away like anything. It sounds just like someone blowing up a bicycle tyre."

Mr. Brown had a problem of his own at that moment without worrying about Paddington making marmalade sandwiches. He had just made the surprising discovery that his face flannel, which he'd left on the balcony outside the room to dry, had completely disappeared and in its place someone had left a very black and oily piece of rag. It was most strange and he couldn't for the life of him think how it could have come about.

Unaware of all the interest he had been causing in the next room, Paddington sat down in the middle of his bedroom floor with a marmalade sandwich in one paw and a large spanner in the other.

On either side of him there were a number of cardboard boxes full of bits and pieces, not to mention a large oilcan, a bicycle pump, and several important-looking tools.

In front of him, looking as clean as a new pin and shiny enough for him to see the reflection of his whiskers on the polished surface, stood a small three-wheeled cycle, and there was a blissful expression on Paddington's face as he took several large bites out of the sandwich and surveyed the result of his evening's work.

Paddington had first seen the tricycle some days before standing in a yard outside a garage at the other end of the village, but until Monsieur Dupont explained about the cycle race that morning he hadn't thought any more about the matter.

The man in the garage had been most surprised when Paddington paid him a visit and at first he had been rather doubtful about hiring the machine to a bear, especially as Paddington had no references apart from some old postcards from his Aunt Lucy.

But Paddington was good at bargaining, and after promising to clean the machine he had at last won the day. The garage man had even lent him the oil-can, which had proved most useful as the tricycle had been standing outside for a number of years and was rather rusty.

Luckily he had found a piece of cloth on the balcony outside Mr. Brown's room and so he'd been able to clean off the worst of the dirt before getting down to the important job of taking it to pieces and polishing it.

All the same, taking the tricycle to pieces had been a lot easier than assembling it again, and as Paddington finished off his sandwich he noticed to his surprise that he had one or two very odd-looking parts left over in the cardboard boxes.

After tying his Union Jack on the handlebars in preparation for the next day, Paddington put the remains of the marmalade sandwiches into the basket on the handle-bars and then climbed on to the saddle with an excited gleam in his eyes.

He had been looking forward to testing the tricycle but as he moved off he soon decided that riding it was much more difficult than it looked, and he began to wish he had longer legs with knees for it was very hard to pedal and sit on the saddle at the same time.

Apart from that, for some reason which he couldn't quite make out, the machine was most difficult to stop no matter what he pulled. Several times he ran into the wardrobe by mistake, and by the time he had finished there were a number of nasty tyre stains on the wall-paper as well. Once, when he rounded a corner at the foot of the bed, the chain came off, nearly throwing him over the handle-bars.

After several more turns round the bedroom Paddington fell off the machine and lay where he was for a few moments mopping his brow with an old handkerchief. Riding tricycles was hot work, especially in such a small space as a hotel bedroom, and after peering at his reflection in the handle-bars once or twice he reluctantly decided to call it a day.

All the same, tired though he was, Paddington found it difficult to get to sleep that night. Apart from the fact that he had to lie on his back with his paws in the air in case any oil came off on the sheets, he had a great many things to think about as well.

But there was a contented expression on his face when he did finally nod off. It had been a good evening's work and he was looking forward to the next day. Paddington felt sure that with such a bright and shiny tricycle he would stand a very good chance indeed of winning a prize in the " Tour de France " cycle race.

The Browns were wakened earlier than usual the next morning by the comings and goings in the square outside the hotel. As if by magic, all the decorations from the *pardon* had suddenly reappeared and the village was full of important-looking men wearing armbands.

There was an air of great excitement and every few minutes a loud-speaker van passed by and addressed the crowd which had collected on the pavement round the square and at the side of the hill leading out of the village.

The Browns had arranged to meet on the balcony outside Paddington's room from where there was a fine view of the hill, but to their surprise when they gathered there Paddington himself was nowhere to be seen.

"I do hope he won't be long," said Mrs. Brown. "He'll be most upset if he misses any of it."

"I wonder where on earth he can have got to?" said Mr. Brown. "I haven't seen him since breakfast."

"H'mm!" said Mrs. Bird, as she looked around the room. "I have my suspicions."

Mrs. Bird's sharp eyes had already noticed the remains of some hastily removed tyre tracks on the floor. They went round the room several times and then out through the door before finally disappearing in the direction of some stairs which led to the back door of the hotel.

Fortunately for Paddington, before Mrs. Bird had time to say any more there was a burst of clapping from the crowd on the pavement below, and so the subject was forgotten as the Browns looked over the balcony to see what was happening.

" How very odd," said Mrs. Brown, as the clapping grew louder and several people cheered. " They seem to be pointing at us."

The Browns became more and more mystified as they waved back at the crowd.

" I wonder what they mean by ' Vive le Bear '? " said Mr. Brown. " It can't be anything to do with Paddington—he isn't here."

" Goodness only knows," said Mrs. Brown. " I suppose we shall just have to wait and see."

Had they but known, the Browns weren't the only ones to wonder what was going on at that moment, but fortunately for their peace of mind there were several streets and a large number of houses between them and the cause of all the excitement.

At the other end of the village Paddington was even more puzzled at the way things were going. In fact, the more he tried to think about the matter the more confused he became. One moment he had been sitting quietly on his tricycle in a side street, peering round the corner every now and then and checking the marmalade sandwiches in the basket on his handle-bars as he waited for the race to appear.

The next moment, as the first of the riders came in sight and he pedalled out to join them, everything seemed to go wrong at once.

Before he knew where he was Paddington found himself caught up in a whirlpool of bicycles and shouting people and policemen and bells.

He pedalled as hard as he could and raised his hat to several of the other cyclists, but the harder he pedalled and the more he raised his hat the louder they shouted and waved back at him, and by then it was much too late to change his mind and turn back even if he'd tried.

Everywhere he looked there were bicycles and men in shorts and striped shirts. There were bicycles in front of him. There were bicycles to the left and bicycles to the right of him. Paddington was much too busy pedalling for dear life to look back, but he was sure there were bicycles behind him as well because he could hear heavy breathing and the sound of bells ringing.

In the excitement someone handed him a bottle of milk as he went past, and in trying to take the bottle with one paw and raise his hat with the other, Paddington had to let go of the handle-bars. He went twice round a statue in the middle of the street before joining the stream of cyclists once more as they swept round a corner on to a road leading out of the village.

Luckily the road was uphill and most of the other cyclists were tired after their long ride, so that by standing on the pedals and jumping up and down as fast as he could he was able to keep up with them.

It was as they reached the top of the hill and rounded another corner leading back down into the village that things suddenly took a decided turn for

the worse. Just as he was about to sit back on the saddle and have a rest while he got his second wind, Paddington found to his surprise that without even having to turn the pedals he was beginning to gather speed.

In fact he hardly had time to wave to the crowd before he found himself starting to overtake the riders in front. He passed one, then another, and then a whole bunch. The cyclists looked quite startled as Paddington flashed by, and all the time the cheering from the spectators on the side of the road grew louder. Quite a number recognised him and they called out words of encouragement, but by then Paddington was much too worried to notice.

He tried pulling as hard as he could on the brake lever but nothing happened, in fact if anything he seemed to go faster than ever and he began to wish he hadn't used quite so much oil on the moving parts when he'd cleaned them.

By then the pedals were going round so fast that he sat back on the saddle and hurriedly lifted up his feet in case his legs fell off.

It was as he gave the brake lever an extra hard pull that he had his second big shock of the day, for it suddenly came away in his paw. Paddington rang his bell frantically and waved the lever as he overtook the last of the riders in front.

" Apply your brakes, Monsieur le Bear! " yelled a man in English as he recognised the Union Jack on Paddington's handle-bars.

" I don't think I can," cried Paddington, looking most upset as he shot past. " My lever's come off in my paw by mistake and I think I've left some of the bits in my box at the hotel! "

Paddington clung to the handle-bars of his tricycle as he hurtled on down the hill towards the village

square. All the villagers were most excited when they saw who was in the lead and a great cheer went up as he came into view, but as he lifted the brim of his hat and peered out anxiously all Paddington could make out was a sea of white faces and a blurred picture of some buildings looming up ahead which he didn't like the look of at all.

But if Paddington was worried the Browns were even more alarmed.

" Good heavens ! " exclaimed Mr. Brown. " It's Paddington ! "

" He's heading straight for Monsieur Dupont's shop," cried Mrs. Brown.

" I can't watch," said Mrs. Bird, closing her eyes.

" Why on earth doesn't he put his brakes on ? " exclaimed Mr. Brown.

" Crikey ! " exclaimed Jonathan. " He can't ! His brake lever's come off ! "

It was Monsieur Dupont himself who saved Paddington. Right at the very last moment his voice rose above the roar of the crowd.

" This way, Monsieur le Bear," he cried, as he flung open the big double gates at the side of his shop. " This way ! "

And before the astonished gaze of the onlookers Paddington shot through them and disappeared from view.

As the rest of the cyclists sped past unheeded the crowd surged forward and gathered round Monsieur Dupont's shop. The Browns only just managed to force their way through to the front before a gasp went up from everyone as a small white figure came into view through the doors.

Even Paddington looked very worried when he saw his reflection in Monsieur Dupont's window and he pinched himself several times to make sure he was all right before raising his hat to the crowd, revealing a small round patch of brown fur.

" I'm not a ghost," he explained, when all the cheering had died down. " I think I must have landed on one of Mr. Dupont's sacks of flour ! "

And as the crowd gathered round Paddington to shake him by the paw, Monsieur Dupont echoed the feelings of them all.

" We of St. Castille," he cried, " shall remember for many years to come the day the ' Tour de France ' passed through our village."

There was a great deal of celebrating in the village

that evening and everyone applauded when the mayor announced that he was giving Paddington a special prize, with as many buns as he could manage into the bargain.

"Not for the fastest rider *through* the village," he said, amid cheers and laughter, "but certainly for the fastest down the hill! We are very proud that someone from our village should have won the prize."

Even Admiral Grundy called in at the hotel especially to congratulate him. "Glad to see you're keepin' the old flag flyin', bear," he said approvingly.

Prddington felt very pleased with himself as he sat up in bed that night surrounded by buns. Apart from having one paw in a sling he was beginning to feel stiff after all his pedalling, and there were still traces of flour left on his fur despite several baths.

But as the mayor had explained, it was the first time he could remember a bear winning a prize in the "Tour de France" cycle race and it was something to be proud of.

The next morning the Browns were up early again for it was time to start their journey back to England. To their surprise everyone else in the village seemed to be up as well in order to send them on their way.

Monsieur Dupont was the last to say good-bye and he looked very sad as the Browns made to leave. "It will seem quiet without you, Monsieur le Bear," he said, shaking Paddington by the paw. " But I hope we shall meet again one day."

" I hope so too, Mr. Dupont," said Paddington earnestly, as he waved good-bye and climbed into the car.

Although he was looking forward to being back home again and to telling Mr. Gruber all about his adventures abroad, Paddington felt very sorry at having to say good-bye to everyone, especially Monsieur Dupont.

" All good things come to an end sooner or later," said Mrs. Brown, as they drove away. " And the nicer it is the sooner it seems to end."

" But if they didn't end," said Mrs. Bird wisely,

" we shouldn't have other things to look forward to."

Paddington nodded thoughtfully as he peered out of the car window. He had enjoyed his holiday in France no end, but it *was* nice knowing that each day brought something new.

" That's the best of being a bear," said Mrs. Bird. " Things happen to bears."